DEA...
DO US
PART

PHIL M. WILLIAMS

AETHON THRILLS

aethonbooks.com

DEATH DO US PART
©2024 PHIL M. WILLIAMS

This book is protected under the copyright laws of the United States of America. No part of this publication may be reproduced, stored in a retrieval system, or transmitted, in any form or by any means, without the prior permission in writing of the publisher, nor be otherwise circulated in any form of binding or cover other than that in which it is published and without a similar condition including this condition being imposed on the subsequent purchaser. Any reproduction or unauthorized use of the material or artwork contained herein is prohibited without the express written permission of the authors.

Aethon Books supports the right to free expression and the value of copyright. The purpose of copyright is to encourage writers and artists to produce the creative works that enrich our culture.

The scanning, uploading, and distribution of this book without permission is a theft of the author's intellectual property. If you would like to use material from the book (other than for review purposes), please contact editor@aethonbooks.com. Thank you for your support of the author's rights.

Aethon Books
www.aethonbooks.com

Print and eBook formatting and design by Steve Beaulieu.

Published by Aethon Books LLC.

Aethon Books is not responsible for websites (or their content) that are not owned by the publisher.

This book is a work of fiction. Names, characters, places, and incidents are the product of the author's imagination or are used fictitiously. Any resemblance to actual events, locales, or persons, living or dead is coincidental.

All rights reserved.

A NOTE FROM PHIL

Dear Reader,

If you're interested in receiving two of my popular thriller novels for free and/or reading many of my other titles for free or discounted, go to the following link: http://www.PhilWBooks.com.

You're probably thinking, *What's the catch?* There is no catch.

Sincerely,

Phil M. Williams

ONE
CRIMINOLOGY 101

"NATURE VERSUS NURTURE. This debate among criminologists still rages today." James surveyed his cozy classroom of undergraduates.

Several coeds in the front row hung on his every word.

James wasn't a stranger to female attention. He had just turned forty, but he was still in decent shape and a dead ringer for Hugh Grant. Not that his students had ever heard of Hugh Grant.

"Raise your hand if you believe that criminals are more likely to be created by societal factors than by biology," James said.

Nearly the entire class of thirty-one students raised their hands.

"Raise your hand if you think biology plays a bigger role than society in creating criminals."

Only two students in the back raised their hands.

"There are plenty of societal factors we could cite to explain criminality." James ticked off each factor on his fingers. "Domestic violence, broken homes, poor schooling, poverty, racism, unemployment, and exposure to gang violence and other crime in the community."

Many of the students nodded along with James's explanation.

James paced in front of his whiteboard. "Criminality is caused by society *and* biology, but biology is actually more indicative of a person's likelihood to commit crime." James paused for effect. "Crime is and has always been a young man's game. In the US, men are four to six times more likely to be arrested than women. Eighteen-year-old males are two to four times as likely to commit a crime as forty-year-old males."

A girl with pink hair raised her hand.

James gestured to the girl. "Yes, Lana."

"It could be that toxic masculinity is taught to boys and not girls," Lana said. "Boys are expected to fight and be aggressive. They're not supposed to show emotions. The patriarchy trains boys to be little psychos."

A spattering of laughter came from some of the students.

"Currently there isn't any data to back up your claim. And, if you look at crime rates among different cultures around the world, and throughout history, you find the same phenomenon. Crime is a young man's game. If, as you claim, crime is a result of toxic masculinity foisted on boys by the patriarchy, then you should see more equal crime rates between the sexes in more egalitarian societies, such as modern-day Sweden, but that's not the case, especially when it comes to violent crime."

Lana crossed her arms over her chest. "Sweden is still a patriarchy."

"It may be that both toxic masculinity and the patriarchy contribute to criminality, but we don't have that data. It would make a great project though. Hint. Hint." James smiled at Lana, letting her know her opinion was valued.

James had learned to be more tactful and considerate of his students since the *incident*, especially regarding the funky-hair crowd. Last year, James had triggered his class during a discussion on the "Central Park Karen." The video of a white woman calling the police on a black man for alleged threats had been viewed on Twitter forty million times. The internet had condemned the woman almost unanimously. His 100 percent Caucasian class had been 100 percent in favor of Amy Cooper losing her job and being imprisoned for filing a false police report.

James had personally thought both Amy Cooper and Christian Cooper—no relation—had acted poorly. This particular incident had interested James because there was such widespread support for Christian Cooper and equally widespread disdain for Amy Cooper, despite some troubling details.

James had challenged his class to think deeper about the incident. "Imagine you're in the middle of a pandemic, and you take your dog to the park because he's full of energy. You let him off the leash to run because he's tugging on the leash nearly choking himself, and nobody else is around. Besides, he's a nice dog who's never bitten anyone. However, it's against the rules of the park to let your dog off his leash. So, little Fido's running around, having a great time, and then a large man appears and asks you to leash your dog because Fido's scaring the birds. Would you leash your dog and move on, or would you defy the man?"

Most of the class had said they would leash their dog and move on. James hadn't shared his opinion, but he would've leashed his dog too.

"For those of you who wouldn't listen to this large stranger, now imagine that he says, 'Look, if you're going to do what you want, I'm going to do what I want, but you're not going to like it.' Then he removes a dog treat from his pocket and beckons your dog. What do you do?"

One blue-haired coed had said, "I wouldn't call the police and ask them to kill the guy."

"Is that what she said?" James had asked.

"Might as well have," another student had said.

"Thankfully we have video, so we know exactly what she said. She approached him and said, 'I'm gonna call the cops. I'm gonna tell them there's an African American man threatening my life.' Then she called 911 and said, 'I'm in the Ramble. There is a man, African-American. He has a bicycle helmet, and he is recording me and threatening me and my dog.'"

"That's the same thing as asking them to kill him," the blue-haired coed had said.

"Do you believe that an accusation of a verbal threat would cause the police to shoot this man?"

"It might."

"Black men get shot for a lot less," another student had said.

"By the numbers, that's unlikely. However, even if the police are unlikely to kill this man, arrest is still a very traumatic situation." James had hesitated for a beat. "Another thing to consider. Christian Cooper admitted to NBC that he brought dog treats with him to the park specifically because it makes dog owners leash their dogs. Show of hands. How many people think Amy had thought Christian might poison her dog?"

Two hands rose tentatively from the back.

"It may be that Amy Cooper is every bit the racist the internet believes that she is, but there might be more to the story here. It's easy to let click-bait headlines and social-media hiveminds trigger your emotions but, as thinking people, we owe it to the world to dig deeper."

This discussion had led to several students reporting James for racism, triggering language, and for making them feel unsafe in his classroom. He had been disciplined with an unpaid suspension.

James continued with the present-day discussion, regarding age and sex differences in crime rates. "Crime often has an aggressive element, and there is data that shows that the average male is more aggressive than the average female. Furthermore, this same aggressiveness disparity can be found in our closest nonhuman ancestors—apes and monkeys."

James paced in front of his class, detailing studies regarding twins and criminality, showing that identical twins were more likely to have similar criminal records than fraternal twins. He then cited several studies involving adoptive boys, which determined that the criminality of the biological parents was a bigger factor in the criminality of the child than the adoptive parents.

Some correlation existed between the criminality of the adoptive parents and the adopted child, but it wasn't as strong as the biological component, suggesting nature and nurture determined criminality, but nature was a stronger determinate.

"No one believes in *crime genes*, but certain attributes that influence criminality—primarily intelligence and temperament—are both inheritable. Studies going back to the 1930s found that the average criminal offender scored 91 to 93 on IQ tests. The general population average is 100, suggesting that lower-than-average IQ increases the likelihood of criminality. This is a nuclear topic among criminologists. Many criminologists dismiss the association between low IQ and criminality."

James explained the alternate theories for the correlation. Low socioeconomic status. Culturally biased IQ tests. Higher IQ offenders less likely to be caught and, therefore, less likely to be reflected in the studies.

"Temperament is also linked to criminal behavior. For those of you who know people involved in crime, I want you to think about them. I want you to think about whether or not they fit any of these characteristics in regard to temperament." James made eye contact with various students. "Criminals tend to be impulsive. They're insensitive to social standards. They lack strong emotional attachments to others, and they have an appetite for danger. Does that sound like anyone you know?"

"Sounds like my entire dorm," said a young man in the back.

The class laughed. So did James.

A petite blonde raised her hand. "What about sociopaths? Are all criminals sociopaths?"

"No. A higher percentage of sociopaths are criminals than the general population, but not all criminals are sociopaths. A sociopath is someone without a conscience. Many criminals were simply young and aggressive at the time of their offense, but once they age and mature, they feel real remorse for their crimes."

"How many people are sociopaths?"

"Estimates vary. Nobody knows for certain. If you believe Dr. Martha Stout, it's about 4 percent of the population."

Many students were wide-eyed and slack-jawed, no doubt doing the math and figuring the probability.

James spelled it out for those who hadn't figured it out. "Based on those numbers, every one of us has at least one sociopath who's close to us."

TWO
THE BIRTHDAY GIRL

AFTER HIS MORNING CLASS, James drove his Honda Accord to Walmart, which was sadly the nearest place to buy books. He browsed the mystery section of the paperbacks, finally settling on *Local Woman Missing* by Mary Kubica. On the way back, he stopped at Desserts Etc. and picked up a birthday cake.

James slowed on US 422 as he puttered into the town of Annville, Pennsylvania. His Honda's automatic transmission was slow to shift gears. James figured the transmission was going on his ten-year-old car, but he thought it would make it through the spring semester, and he could get it fixed in the summer.

Rowhouses lined the streets, occupied by restaurants, bars, antique stores, furniture stores, and a natural food market. He stopped at the single stoplight. Sunlight filtered through his windows, heating the interior of his vehicle.

The light went green, and he drove past the gas station and the Turkey Hill convenience store. He passed the Allen Theatre, a quaint cinema and coffee shop that James and his wife, Rachel, frequented. He turned left onto College Avenue and the campus of Lebanon Valley College, then parked near the admissions building.

James grabbed the birthday cake that read *Happy Birthday, Liv* and carried it along a concrete path. The grass had been freshly mowed with perfect green stripes, the first cut of the spring season. Even without their leaves, trees provided dappled shade with their thick branches and beauty with their buds. The main campus was arranged in a rectangle, with brick buildings surrounding a grassy courtyard. The outskirts featured apartment-like dormitories and sports fields.

James walked into the three-story redbrick building that housed the admissions and financial aid offices. He balanced the cake and the mystery novel in one hand, like a waiter, as he hefted the ornate door. He made a beeline for the admissions office.

The young receptionist smiled at James and said, "Hi, Professor Harris."

James smiled back. "Is Liv in?"

"She's in her office." The receptionist eyed the cake. "Is it her birthday?"

James put his finger to his lips. "It's a surprise."

"That's so sweet," she whispered.

James breezed past the reception area to Liv's office. The placard on her door read *Olivia Wallace, Office of Admissions*. She was the assistant to the head of admissions, which meant she did all the work for half the pay.

James knocked on the door.

"Come in," Liv called out.

James entered her cramped office. "Happy birthday."

Liv stood from her seat, beaming. "You didn't have to get me anything."

James set the cake on her desk, then handed her the book. "What are friends for?"

Liv took the book and studied the cover.

"I hope you haven't read that one yet," James said. Liv was an avid reader of mysteries, but she usually waited for new novels to be discounted as mass market paperbacks or dirt-cheap e-books.

"I've been waiting for this one to go on sale. I almost broke down and paid fourteen bucks for the e-book. I'm glad I didn't. Thank you, James."

He winked and said, "You have any plates and utensils?"

Liv found paper plates and plastic forks and invited her coworkers to share her cake. After her coworkers took their cake slivers to their workstations, Liv shut her door and sat across from James at her desk. "I really shouldn't be eating this," Liv said, just before taking a bite.

"It's your birthday," James replied, just before taking a bite.

She swallowed, then pointed her plastic fork at her cake. "This is so good, but I need to lose some weight."

James frowned. "You look great." If James took a lie detector test, he would've failed. What was he supposed to say? *Cheer up. Most thirty-five-year-old Americans are chubby. It's no big deal.* Truth be told, if judging from a superficial perspective, Liv was the epitome of average. Average height, straight brown hair to her shoulders, oval frameless glasses, and an oversized beige sweater to minimize her extra pounds.

Liv blushed. "I almost believed you. You're a good liar."

"You *do* look great."

Liv rolled her eyes. "Then why am I forever single?"

"Men are stupid." James took another bite of cake.

"I think I'll live in your delusion for a while. It feels good."

"You just need to put yourself out there. I hear you and Rachel are going out on the town tonight. Maybe you'll meet someone."

Rachel and Liv were best friends since grade school. Two years after high school, Liv went to work at Lebanon Valley College as a receptionist while Rachel was an undergraduate pursuing a degree in psychology. James had been a young professor of criminology at the time. When James and Rachel recounted their *how we met story*, they always credited Liv with introducing them. It was much more palatable than the truth. Rachel had been in James's criminal behavior class. They hid their relationship for almost two years, until Rachel graduated. They married in the second year of Rachel's doctoral program.

Liv creased her brow for an instant, as if she had forgotten her birthday plans with Rachel. Then she said, "It should be fun, but I'm not the best at putting myself out there."

James stabbed the last of his cake with his plastic fork. "The first step is not giving a shit about what anyone thinks about you."

"When you grow up in a small town, you care about what *everyone* thinks."

"Rachel grew up in the same town as you, and I'm pretty sure she doesn't give a shit about anyone's opinion, including mine."

"The same rules don't apply to goddesses." Liv stared at the last scrap of her birthday cake.

James laughed. "Don't tell her that. She might make me worship her and offer up my blood as a sacrifice."

"You laugh, but everybody already worships her. You have to see that." Liv ate the last of her cake.

"People *like* her, but *worship*'s a bit strong."

Liv set down her fork, her plate now clean. "Trust me. It's worship. Did she ever tell you about the time she got three boys to jump into the quarry?"

James leaned forward in his seat. "*No.* What happened?"

"It was the summer before our junior year. Rachel had just gotten her driver's license. Her dad bought her a brand-new Jeep."

"I heard about the Jeep."

"She invited these three boys to go to the quarry with us. They were in love with her. She made it seem like she was into them too. One of them was the quarterback on the football team, the most popular boy at school. Another was his teammate, a big lineman who went to Penn State on a scholarship."

"What about the other guy?" James asked.

"He shouldn't have been there. You know my cousin Damon."

"Vaguely. Doesn't he work for Taylor Construction?"

Taylor Construction was founded by Rachel's father and currently managed by Rachel's twin brother.

"Since he was eighteen." Liv let out a heavy breath. "Anyway, when we got there, we walked out to the ledge—have you ever been to the quarry?"

"No. I haven't."

"It's been closed for a long time. I think it was a marble quarry. There's a lake or a pond or whatever at the bottom of the pit. You can jump into the lake in a bunch of spots, but the ledge we went to was really high, like ten stories, maybe higher. Nobody ever jumped from there."

James nodded.

"We were looking over the edge and messing around, acting like we were gonna push each other off, but none of us would've really done that, you know?"

James nodded again, concerned about the direction of the story.

"So Rachel told the guys that, if they jumped, she'd kiss them. Mr. Popular was like, 'We need more than a kiss for that.'" Liv mimicked a man's voice. "Rachel played along, asking him what he wanted. Then the big lineman interrupted them and said *they* wanted a blow job, as if he was speaking for all the guys."

James cringed, definitely not liking where this story was going.

Liv continued. "So Rachel tells them that, if they want a blow job, they have to strip *and* jump in the quarry. The two football players went to the edge again and looked, like really looked, and they were scared. Then Damon said, 'I just want a kiss.' And he jumped."

"Wow."

Liv nodded, a small smile on her lips. "I know. We all looked over the edge, and Damon didn't come up for like ten seconds, but it felt like a lot longer. Then he came up and shook his fist. Damon was one of those awkward kids who always got picked on, but he was braver than those two jocks. I was so proud of him."

"What happened next? Did the other guys jump?"

"After seeing it wasn't that dangerous, they stripped, like bare-ass stripped, and they both jumped together, like they were Thelma and Louise or some shit." Liv giggled. "Then Rachel took their clothes, and we went back to the Jeep and drove away."

James furrowed his brow. "You left them?"

Liv touched her chest. "*I* didn't leave them. Your wife was the one with the Jeep."

"How did they get home?"

Liv shrugged. "They walked."

"Were they mad?"

"That's why she's a goddess. Even after that, they were all still in love with her."

THREE
THE GODDESS

JAMES DROVE on his curvy gravel driveway through the forest. A one-acre clearing revealed his two-story Cape Cod. The white clapboard siding glowed in the afternoon sun. The house had a gabled roof, dormer windows with black shutters, and a large central chimney. James's garden, orchard, and lawn surrounded his home. The fruit trees bloomed white, pink, and red. The gardens were dark brown, freshly mulched, and ready for planting.

A little red Corvette was parked in the driveway. James stopped his Honda and pressed the garage door opener on his visor. As he waited for the garage door to fully open, movement caught his peripheral vision. He turned. A muscled man with a scruffy beard and a nose like a prize fighter contorted himself into the Corvette. James had never met someone in the Russian Mafia, but if he had, he imagined they would resemble that guy. The big guy had come from the rear walkway, which was the entrance to Rachel's home office.

James drove into his garage, parking next to Rachel's Mercedes. He watched the Corvette disappear in his rearview mirror before shutting the garage door. He exited his Honda, shouldered his laptop bag, and entered the mudroom. The chest freezer hummed in the background, still holding leftover veggies from last fall's harvest and beef from the quarter cow he had purchased from a local farmer. A bench sat along the wall opposite the freezer, with built-in cubbies filled with their shoes. James changed his dress shoes for his slippers, then entered his house.

He walked through the laundry room, then the kitchen and dining room. The decor was quaint and country, with pale-yellow walls, antique wooden furniture, and faux-flower arrangements. He dropped off his laptop bag in his home office, then entered the forbidden area, which was an addition they had added when Rachel started her own practice.

James slipped down the hallway, passing the empty waiting room and the empty exit room. The exit room was decorated with plants and cheerful landscape paintings. A box of tissues sat on the end table, next to the couch. This space was where clients processed and decompressed after an intense psychotherapy session.

Rachel's office door was cracked open a few inches. James pushed inside, barely making a sound. A couch sat against the near wall, facing a chair, the place where the magic happened. Beyond that, Rachel sat at her mahogany desk, thumb-typing on her phone. James stepped to her desk.

Rachel set her phone face down and scowled. "I could've been with a client."

"I saw him leave. I figured it was safe," James replied.

She sighed. "What do you want?"

Even when mildly annoyed, she was irresistible. James didn't know how her male clients could possibly focus on their mental health with this beauty in front of them. Maybe Liv was right. Rachel was a goddess. She had the sophistication of a doctor, with her tailored skirt-suit, heels, and hose, her auburn hair in a tight bun. On the other hand, she had the sex appeal of a Hollywood starlet, with an athletic body, high cheekbones, and a wrinkle-free face that didn't appear much older than James's students.

James grinned. "I thought we could spend some quality time together before dinner."

"I have another appointment in thirty minutes."

James sat in the chair across from her.

"Don't get comfortable," she said.

"It's been a while. A long time actually."

Her phone buzzed. She tilted up her phone, peeking at the notification, then said, "Maybe tomorrow. I need to get back to work."

It used to be, when Rachel prefaced something with *maybe*, especially something sexual, it would likely occur, but she was being coy. Lately, *maybe* meant *unlikely* or *when hell freezes over*.

Her phone buzzed again.

James gestured to her phone. "Is that Liv?"

Rachel peeked at her phone again, hesitated for a beat, then said, "Yes, *um*, she just wanted to confirm the time for tonight."

"I stopped by admissions and wished Liv a happy birthday. I brought her a book and a cake from Desserts Etc."

Rachel rolled her eyes. "She must've loved that."

James held out his hands. "What?"

"You know what. She loves attention from you."

"She's *your* friend. I'm the friend-in-law."

"Doesn't mean she's not in love with you."

"Stop. You don't know that. She's never said or done anything inappropriate."

"You forget who you're talking to. I know Liv like the back of my hand. She's always been hot for my boyfriends, and she's been in love with you for fifteen years."

James leaned back, his forehead creased. "Come on, Rachel. You don't know that for sure."

"Yes, I do. She won't admit it, but I see the way she lights up when she sees you. She doesn't need you being nice to her. She needs to move on. I can't remember the last time she's even had a date."

Fifteen years ago, James met Liv one month before Rachel. He had been friendly, maybe even flirty with Liv, but he'd had no intentions outside of friendship. According to Rachel, Liv had a crush on James back then and was heartbroken when Rachel told Liv about her secret affair with Professor Harris.

"What am I supposed to do? Ignore her?" James asked.

Rachel shrugged. "You could stop being so nice to her."

"This is ridiculous. I can't believe we're having this discussion again."

"I can't believe you keep stringing her along to pump up your ego."

James was speechless for a moment. "Are you trying to pick a fight?"

"I need you to leave. I have a session soon, and I can't be in this negative headspace."

"How come you never told me about manipulating those boys to jump into the quarry?"

It was her turn to be speechless for a moment. "I don't have to tell you everything that's ever happened in my lifetime."

"They could've died."

Rachel snickered. "Now you're being overly dramatic. I've seen plenty of people jump into the quarry. I've jumped in myself."

"Not from that height."

Rachel shook her head. "According to who? Liv? She's an exaggerator. Nobody was injured." Rachel pointed toward the exit. Her voice was calm and even, her therapy voice. "We can talk about this later, if you must, but I need you to leave."

The doorbell chimed.

James stood from his chair. "Liv and I are friends. That's it."

"I know *you* know that."

James flashed his palms. "I'll keep my distance, if that's what you want."

"It's not what *I* want. It's what *she* needs."

"Okay. What time do you think you'll be home tonight? I could wait up."

"It'll be late. I would rather not keep you up. On a side note, don't forget that we have dinner at my brother's tomorrow."

"I didn't forget." James tapped his head. "Mind like a steel trap."

As he turned and left the office, Rachel called out to his back, "I love you."

"Love you too."

The doorbell chimed again.

James went to the front door, thinking about what Rachel had said. James did enjoy the sexual tension with Liv, even if it never went anywhere, and he did like her as a friend, but maybe he *was* holding her back. Maybe he *was* the reason she was still single. James opened the door to the postman.

He signed for the postal delivery and took the small-but-heavy box. It was the coins he had ordered. James also scooped up several FedEx boxes that had been delivered earlier that day. They were all for Rachel, likely clothes or shoes or some high-end health and beauty products. It wasn't uncommon for Rachel to receive multiple packages each week.

James went inside, set the FedEx packages on the kitchen counter, and took his box to his office. He set it on his desktop and opened it with a box cutter. Inside were several rolls of Silver American Eagles. James saved in gold and silver. Knowing the history of money, he didn't trust banks or fiat currencies. As Voltaire once wrote, *Paper money eventually returns to its intrinsic value—zero.*

Every month James spent eight hundred dollars on silver coins, automatically deducted from his account and shipped to his house. At the end of each year, if he had any additional savings, he purchased gold coins. Rachel had lobbied to sell his gold and silver on many occasions, preferring to enjoy the money now versus saving for the future, but James had refused.

He knelt beneath his desk and pressed on a wooden panel. The panel opened, revealing a secret compartment and a safe inside. He worked the combination and opened the safe. It was packed to the gills with gold and silver coins and bars, worth approximately $500,000.

FOUR
MAYBE

JAMES TOSSED AND TURNED, thinking about his argument with Rachel. Was that why they hadn't had sex in months? Did she think he was too flirty with Liv? James doubted that. Rachel had never been jealous of Liv. Maybe Rachel really believed that James was holding Liv back from dating.

Until recently, maybe the last four months, James and Rachel's sex life had always been healthy. More than healthy even. Rachel had been insatiable and adventurous early in their relationship, when she had been an undergrad and their relationship was a dirty secret. She was like a drug, and James had been an addict.

It hadn't been uncommon for James to wake up with Rachel giving him a blow job, or even riding him, taking advantage of his morning wood. James was lucky he hadn't been fired for some of her antics. Rachel had flashed him in class, sitting in the front row in her skirt, with nothing underneath, and opening her legs. She had attended his office hours too, still wearing her skirt, waiting for the last student to leave so they could fuck.

Rachel had enjoyed role play too. They'd driven into Harrisburg and had gone to some bar separately, and James would try to pick her up. He never knew who she'd be, and she never broke character. She'd be a different person, which had only heightened his arousal for her. They had started with the ditzy stewardess on a layover. It had been a cliché, but she'd been fun and easy. She'd had a flight to catch, so the time limit had added to the excitement. Rachel had even worn a stewardess uniform for the occasion.

They had turned up the heat with the married woman on the prowl, looking to settle the score with her philandering husband. She'd been easy and dirty, begging for all the things her husband no longer gave her. It felt so real that James had been worried that some guy who Rachel had hired to play the husband might barge into their hotel room.

James had tried to play different characters himself, but he was terrible at it and it only made the pickup more difficult, so he usually played an unmarried version of himself.

One of their favorite characters had been Sarah, a twenty-one-year-old virgin who had just found out that her devout Christian fiancé had slept with her best friend. "Sarah" had even worn cheap conservative clothes from Target for the occasion. She had worn little makeup, her hair in a simple ponytail with a scrunchy. Even though Rachel had tried to *not* look sexy, it made her even sexier.

Sarah wouldn't be caught dead in a bar by herself, so they'd gone to out-of-town grocery stores to stage the introduction. James had pretended to shop. Sarah had really shopped, and, when she came to the register, she had been distraught that she didn't have enough cash, forcing her to set aside items. James had played the hero, offering to cover her bill. Sarah had always declined his offer initially, but, with some witty banter and coaxing, Sarah had usually accepted.

In the parking lot, James had offered to help her load her groceries, which, after some coaxing, she'd also accepted. After loading her groceries, Sarah had often driven away alone and the game would be over, unless James had charmed her. In fact, they had played four times before James even got a kiss.

James had broken the ice with witty banter and some funny

but tasteful jokes. He had coaxed her into a walk. It had been a nice night. They had strolled along the nearby river, then they had sat on a bench. He had been a shoulder for her to cry on about her fiancé. Rachel's performance had been so real. Sarah had been so vulnerable and naive. James had kissed her, and it was electric, like kissing another woman for the first time, until she had slapped him, called him a creep, and ran back to her car.

At home, James had asked Rachel what they were doing. They hadn't had sex in two weeks, since they had been playing the "Sarah" game.

Rachel had replied cryptically, "If you want Sarah, you have to take charge."

This went on for another two weeks. They kept meeting at various grocery stores, and James kept striking out with Sarah. In the meantime, Rachel hadn't been sleeping with him, so James's desire for Sarah increased. Soon his thoughts had been flooded with fantasies of Sarah.

After a month without sex, James had been practically foaming at the mouth with desire for her, but he knew that wouldn't win the prize. So he had played it cool. They had returned to the grocery store by the river. He had been witty. He had cheered her up. He had been the perfect gentleman. They had talked for hours on a bench overlooking the river. Sarah had cried and thanked him and laid her head on his shoulder. She had even kissed his cheek, but James hadn't even put his arm around her.

Sarah had always used the excuse that her ice cream was melting, like the stewardess with a flight, also giving their interaction a time limit. Time to go home in their separate cars. Another failure.

On the stroll back to their cars, James had said, "I don't want this night to end."

"Me neither," Sarah had said.

"My house is nearby, if you want to spend more time together."

Sarah had taken a step away from James. "I don't think that's a good idea. I barely know you."

Then James had realized "Sarah" would never sleep with some guy she met at a grocery store on the first night. James had finally realized what Rachel had meant when she said, "If you want Sarah, you have to take charge."

The grocery store had just closed, and their cars were the last two in the parking lot. Like a gentleman, James had accompanied Sarah to her car. He'd kissed her too, not getting too handsy.

When they separated, Sarah had been blushing. "I should go." She turned to leave, and James grabbed her wrist. "What are you doing?" she had asked, her eyes wide open.

James had gestured to her back seat. "Get in the back."

She had struggled, twisting her arm and planting her feet, but James had overpowered her and shoved her into her back seat. In the back seat of her car, in the middle of a deserted grocery store parking lot, he had ripped her cheap cotton underwear, lifted her dress, and took what he wanted. Sarah had begged and cried real tears, but James felt the truth. Rachel had never been wetter. Rachel had never come so hard. And neither had James.

After James had cracked the code, the game had gotten even more perverse. One night, James had held Sarah at gunpoint with a replica revolver, forcing her into her car, then forcing her to drive home. At home, he had wanted to take her without fear of someone seeing them, then having to have the awkward *It's just role play* conversation. But Sarah hadn't made it easy.

As soon as he had parked in the garage, Sarah had exited the car and had run down the driveway, screaming for help. James had sprinted after her, tackling her in the woods, and taking her on the forest floor.

It had been many years since they had been that adventurous.

The garage door motored up. The throaty V-8 of Rachel's Mercedes pulled into the garage. James glanced at the clock on their bedside table—*2:26 a.m.* Almost every bar in the area closed by midnight. The garage door motored down.

Shortly thereafter, Rachel tiptoed upstairs. She must've skipped the second step, as that one always creaked. She crept down the hallway and into their bedroom. James turned on the bedside table lamp.

Rachel stopped in her tracks, wearing a short corduroy skirt, a low-cut blouse, and smoky eye makeup. "You're still up?" Rachel asked.

James held out his hand. "Come to bed. I've missed you."

"I need to shower. I smell like smoke."

"I don't care. I want you."

"Maybe after my shower." She pivoted and walked to their master bathroom.

Her smell hung in the air for second, but it wasn't smoke. It was cologne.

FIVE
THE ABYSS

JAMES MADE a late Saturday morning breakfast, hoping Rachel would awaken to the smell of coffee and bacon, but she never did. With breakfast getting cold on the table, James went to their master bedroom, carrying her coffee—with two stevia packets and cream, just the way she liked it.

Rachel slept on her side, near the edge of their king-size sleigh bed. Without makeup, her face appeared younger, innocent, maybe even more beautiful.

James bent down near her face, the coffee wafting into her nostrils, and said, "Breakfast is ready."

Her eyelids fluttered open, and she recognized James. She rolled to her back and stretched her arms upward. "I'm not hungry."

James noticed a dark mark on her cheekbone, near her eye. He thought it was probably smudged makeup.

Rachel sat upright and held out her hands. "But I'll take that coffee."

James handed her the coffee, getting a better look at that smudge, realizing it was a bruise.

Rachel sipped her coffee.

James asked, "What happened to your face?"

"Oh, this?" she asked, touching the bruise on her face while still holding her coffee in her opposite hand.

"What happened? Are you okay?"

Rachel smirked. "It's nothing. If I tell you what happened, will you promise not to laugh at me?" She sipped her coffee again.

"Why would I laugh at you?"

"Because it's *really* dumb. I actually walked into the doorframe of my office. I should do a PSA about the dangers of texting and walking."

James narrowed his eyes. "Are you sure you're okay? You want some ice?"

Rachel set her coffee on the bedside table, flipped the comforter off her body, and exited the bed. She wore a white t-shirt that hung just below her cotton underwear. She squeezed James's hand and said, "I'm fine. Don't worry about me." She left James for the master bathroom.

James followed her like a puppy dog, talking to her back. "You want me to put your breakfast in the fridge?"

She went into the bathroom, then the water closet, and shut the door behind her.

As she peed, James stood on the white tile, just outside the water closet. "We need to talk."

No response came from Rachel. Only the *whoosh* of her urine. She flushed the toilet, exited the water closet, and walked to the his-and-hers sinks.

Again, James followed her. "We need to talk."

Rachel washed her hands, looking at James in the mirror. "I'm sorry about last night. I know you were in the mood, but I was really tired."

"There's always a reason. It's an issue. It's not just the sex either. I feel like we're drifting apart, especially over the past few months. I'm worried that something's going on."

Rachel dried her hands on the towel and turned to James. "Like what?"

"Like an affair."

Rachel drew back. "An affair? You can't be serious."

James pressed his lips together in a straight line, then said, "You smelled like cologne last night."

Rachel laughed. "Oh, that? I saw my friend Ethan, from high school. He gave me a hug right before Liv and I left the bar. He must've bathed in that cheap cologne."

James stared at Rachel, not sure whether to believe her. Rachel went to James and pressed her body against his, wrapped her arms around his back, and squeezed for a long time.

When they separated, Rachel said, "I'm sorry. I know I've been neglectful. It's … I'm not supposed to tell you this, but …"

"But what?"

"You said that we've been drifting apart for a few months, right?"

James nodded. "Probably the last three or four months."

"I'm struggling with one of my patients—a man who I started treating about four months ago. I think he really got to me."

"In what way?"

"It's like what Nietzsche said. 'If you stare long enough into the abyss, the abyss will stare back into you.' With this guy, I feel like I'm staring into the eyes of the devil, and it's made me more guarded, less interested in connection with you, with anybody really." Rachel took his hand. "I'm sorry. I'll work through it. This isn't your fault."

James leaned forward and kissed her on the lips. "Don't apologize. I know your work is intense. Did this guy do something to you? Something that scared you?"

"Not directly. He's a raging misogynist who has rape and murder fantasies about his wife, which I listen to in excruciating detail. Yet that's not the scary part." Rachel opened the bathroom drawer and removed the floss. "His first wife died while changing the tire on their car."

"What happened? Did another car hit them?"

Rachel shook her head. "She was underneath the car, and it fell on her."

"That's weird. Was she alone?"

"He was with her."

James knitted his brow. "Why would she even be under the car in the first place? You don't have to get under the car to change a tire, and, even if you did, shouldn't *he* be changing the tire?"

"Exactly. Apparently, his first wife had a generous life insurance policy. Now I'm terrified for his current wife, who's wealthy and fourteen years older than him."

James winced. "That's not good. Why don't you call the police or at least drop him as a client?"

Rachel pulled a strip of floss from the plastic container, cutting the thread with the tiny guillotine-like device. "He hasn't admitted to anything illegal, and, if I drop him now, who knows what might happen. I wouldn't be able to live with myself if I dropped him and then his wife ended up dead."

SIX
COMMIE PROFESSORS

"I'M NOT LOOKING FORWARD to this," James said as they drove through an upscale neighborhood. "Your brother's always worse when we're at his house. I think he's an alcoholic, by the way."

"Just don't talk about politics," Rachel replied.

"He says dumb shit sometimes."

Rachel pointed at her husband. "That's what gets you into trouble. Let him say all the dumb shit he wants."

On their right, an SUV barreled down a driveway. James braked and stopped, anticipating that the SUV would pull out into the street without stopping. The SUV screeched to a halt near the driveway apron.

"What the hell is he doing?" Rachel asked.

"I don't think he saw us," James replied.

The man in the SUV waved to James and beckoned them forward. So James pressed on the gas. The Honda hesitated before lurching forward.

"What's wrong with your car?" Rachel asked.

James waved at the SUV driver, then said, "I think the transmission's going."

"We could've taken my car."

"My car gets better gas mileage, the tires are cheaper, repairs are cheaper."

"*You're* cheap. If we break down, I'm not walking. I'll sit right here and you can push."

This wasn't an insult, nor meant to be. James was proud of his frugality. Rachel found it endearing and quite liked to do the spending.

He grinned. "I'll carry you home, my dear."

James parked his Honda along the street in front of Rachel's brother's house. The late-afternoon sun was low on the horizon, casting the brick-faced McMansion in an orange glow. Two Taylor Construction pickups were parked in the driveway, along with Rachel's father's SUV. One of the pickups was old and abused. The other was brand new, complete with every bell and whistle available on an F-250.

James and Rachel ambled up the driveway, then the brick walkway toward the front door. Rachel carried a bottle of red wine. A small man wearing a backpack sprayer sprayed weeds in the flowerbeds with herbicide.

"Hi, Damon," Rachel said as they neared Liv's cousin.

Damon turned to Rachel as if James didn't exist. He leered at Rachel for a long beat, then said, "Rachel."

"You doing okay? I hope my brother's not working you too hard."

He shrugged, still not acknowledging James. He mumbled something under his breath. To James it sounded like, *Doesn't matter.*

"What was that?" Rachel asked.

"Nothing," Damon replied. Then he turned back to the flowerbed, back to spraying dandelions.

James and Rachel continued to the front door. Rachel pressed the doorbell.

James leaned toward Rachel and whispered into her ear, "What's his problem?"

"I don't know. He's weird sometimes," Rachel whispered back.

Rachel's sister-in-law Michelle answered the door with a smile. "Hey, you two. Come on in."

Michelle's face appeared unnatural when she smiled, the heavy makeup covering any lines or blemishes. The makeup matched her fake blonde hair though.

They followed Michelle to the open-plan kitchen, which was as big as James and Rachel's living room. Rachel's mother, Linda, arranged the side dishes on the center island, buffet style. Even though it wasn't Linda's kitchen, Linda likely did most of the cooking.

"Smells great," James said.

Linda looked up from the food. "Hello, James." Then she addressed Rachel with a warm smile. "Hi, honey."

Linda was short, with a puffy face and bags under her eyes. If he squinted, James could see Rachel's face in there. He wondered if Rachel would look like her mother in twenty-nine years. It was hard to believe Rachel would ever look old, but it happened to everyone.

Rachel and James each hugged Linda.

"The boys are on the deck," Michelle said to James, a not-so-subtle hint that she'd like some girl time with Rachel.

Michelle had a love/hate relationship with Rachel. Michelle had always admired Rachel's beauty, brains, and fashion sense, but Michelle was also insanely jealous. In comparison to most thirty-six-year-old women with two kids, Michelle looked pretty good, but there was no comparison to Rachel. Hence, Michelle often monopolized Rachel, alternately prodding Rachel about having children, as this was one area where Michelle had won, plus bragging about her lavish lifestyle, another area where Michelle had won.

James left the kitchen. He stepped through the family room, speeding his pace when he passed the big-screen television where

Rachel's nephews played some first-person shooter game. "Sorry."

The boys, nine and ten years old, wore their headsets and didn't reply or even seem to notice.

James continued through the sunroom and out to the deck where he found Rachel's fraternal twin, Matt, manning the grill and talking to his father, George. Matt was average height and heavyset, with a second trimester gut. His dirty-blond beard matched his short hair. Matt saw James first, glancing at him, but then continued his conversation with his father. George was overdressed as usual, wearing slacks and a button-down shirt with his trademark suspenders. He was a fit man for his age, with a gray-and-white beard to match his full head of hair.

As James drew nearer, George turned and said, "James. How are you?"

"I'm doing well," James replied.

Matt lifted his chin to James. "Wanna beer?"

George held a beer bottle. Another beer bottle sat on the platform next to the grill, likely some obscure IPA that had been approved by Matt. Rachel's chubby twin was the best beer connoisseur in all of Pennsylvania, if you listened to him.

James held up one hand. "No thanks."

Matt raised one side of his mouth. "You can drink wine with the women." Matt flipped a steak, then pushed on the meat with his spatula, the meat sizzling in response.

———

Forks and knives tapped and scraped the plates in the formal dining room. Taken together, eight people, cutting and stabbing their food, provided for an almost musical ambiance. James took a sip of his red wine, the same wine Rachel had brought, and the same wine Linda and Michelle also drank. James had planned to drink beer with dinner, but, after Matt's sexist comment at the grill, James had decided to drink wine for spite.

Kyle, the older boy, stood from his seat and said, "We're going to play."

Michelle gestured to their half-eaten plates. Neither of them had touched their asparagus. "Take your plates to the sink."

Kyle and Lyle took their plates to the kitchen.

James took a sip from his wineglass. He preferred whiskey, but the wine was smooth.

Matt stared at James in disbelief. "You look like a wine drinker."

"I doubt I want to know what that means," James replied.

James thought Matt was on his fifth beer, not counting any beers he'd had before James and Rachel had arrived.

"Be nice," Michelle warned Matt.

"I'm just saying. He looks like a wine drinker." Matt grabbed his beer bottle and held it with his pinky protruding. He chuckled and said, "You need to hold your pinky like this though."

Michelle gave Matt a look that could kill. "*Stop.*"

"I think that's when you're using a teacup with that little handle," James said matter-of-factly. He sipped his wine again.

"That what they teach you in college?" Matt asked. "How to drink tea and wine? How to know what piece of fancy silverware goes with what dish?"

"That's finishing school."

"I had a girlfriend who went to finishing school," Linda said. "Her family was well-off. Do they even have finishing schools anymore?"

"I think so," James replied.

"This is what happens when you don't have to work for a living," Matt said. "You know about all this gay shit."

"That's enough," George said, his face like stone.

Matt waved him off. "You know what I'm talking about, Dad. You worked for a living. I work for a living. We build houses. Business buildings. That's *working* for a living."

"I don't know why I keep going to work every day and teaching classes and grading papers and doing research and writing," James said. "I wasn't aware that I didn't need to do any of that."

Rachel nudged James. She whispered, "Don't engage."

Matt gestured to James with his beer bottle. "Pushing papers isn't real work. That's the problem with this country. Nobody wants to do any real work. Every year it gets harder and harder to hire labor."

Michelle stood from the table and said to James, "Don't listen to him. He's talking out of his ass again." She picked up her plate, silverware, and wineglass. "I'm going to clean up."

Linda stood from the table too. "I'll help."

Michelle and Linda left.

"We do need more skilled labor," James said to Matt. "You're right about that, but that doesn't mean intellectual work isn't real work. If Americans don't want to do skilled labor, then the rates for that work go higher, and all those hardworking people benefit from higher wages."

Matt grunted. "Yeah. *They* benefit. People like me get squeezed. I got unskilled laborers wanting $25 an hour."

"Wages have to rise until there's an equilibrium."

Matt chugged the last of his beer and slammed it on the table. "You don't like capitalism, do you?"

"I never said anything about capitalism."

George stood from his seat and put his hand on Matt's shoulder. "Maybe you should go up to bed and sleep it off."

Matt glared at his father. "This is *my* house. I'll make that decision."

George frowned. "Suit yourself." He took his plate and left the dining room.

"We should go too." Rachel stood from her seat.

James stood too. "Thanks for dinner, Matt."

Matt sneered at James. "Did you know that 90 percent of professors are leftists?"

"That's probably true," James replied. "Not many conservatives in my profession."

"And 40 percent are socialists. Can you believe that? Fucking commies."

Rachel grabbed her plate. "I'm done with this." She left the dining room.

"That might be true too," James said. "I don't know."

Matt reddened. James's agreement only seemed to anger him further. "You're probably making little commies at LVC."

"Communism is an evil ideology responsible for at least one hundred million deaths in the twentieth century. It's not something I encourage in my classes. It would be akin to encouraging Nazism."

Matt went silent for an instant. Then he said, "You know why professors are commies? Because they don't work for a living. They expect the government to pay for everything. They're leeches."

"I might be offended if I thought you were talking about me. After all, LVC is a private college, therefore leech-free." James grabbed his plate and his gay wineglass. "Thanks for dinner, Matt. Always a pleasure."

SEVEN
BREAKDOWN

JAMES DROVE ON A TWO-LANE ROAD, passing farms and forest, his headlights cutting a path through the darkness. Rachel sat in the front passenger seat, silent, staring out the window.

"Your brother's an asshole," James said.

Rachel didn't respond.

"Every time we go to his house, he gets wasted and acts like some caricature of a redneck Republican. He talks about me pushing papers. I doubt he's doing any manual labor with that beer gut."

Rachel didn't respond.

James gripped the steering wheel, his knuckles white. "I'm not going over there again. I'm out."

Rachel still didn't respond.

James glanced at Rachel, who continued to stare out the window. "Did you hear what I said? I'm done." James glanced at Rachel again. "Rachel?"

She let out a long breath, turned to James, and said, "I told you not to engage."

"So this is my fault? All I did was agree with him."

"That's not what you were doing, and you know it. You were

purposely frustrating him by agreeing with him and enjoying every minute of it."

"So what if I was? I was defending myself in the kindest way possible."

Rachel raised her eyebrows. "Really? By triggering a drunk idiot? By making Matt look stupid? By showing everyone your superior intellect?"

They drove past a subdivision and a church.

"I still don't understand how any of this is my fault. He started it," James said.

"Now you sound like a child," Rachel replied.

"We always fight when we go see your family. That should tell you something."

Rachel glared at James. "Don't you dare bring my parents into this. They didn't do anything."

"They didn't? Remember last summer at the Fourth of July party? Your mom said, and I quote, 'Rachel makes all the money. No wonder he has time to putter around the garden.'"

"*Jesus,* James. She was joking. Do you ever forget anything?"

The car slowed dramatically, as if James had slammed on the brakes, but he hadn't touched the brakes. The car jerked and lurched. The check engine light appeared on the dash.

Rachel braced herself with her hands on the dashboard, which she did anytime she thought they might crash, despite James's admonishments that bracing herself wouldn't save her in a crash. In fact, it might break her arms.

"What's happening?" Rachel screeched.

James pulled over on the gravelly shoulder. "*Shit*. It's the transmission." He cut the engine, pulled the emergency brake, and turned to Rachel. "You want me to carry you home?"

Rachel scowled. "You're unbelievable."

James smiled. "Thanks. I try."

Rachel grabbed her purse and exited the car, slamming the door behind her. James exited too. Rachel marched toward home, which was about one mile away.

James called out, "I guess I'll wait for the tow truck." He watched her until she disappeared around the hairpin turn. Then James called for a tow truck.

"It'll be about three hours," the guy said.

"I'll walk home then," James replied. "I'll leave the keys in the center console."

"That's fine."

"Can you tow it to Scott's Transmission Center in Lebanon?"

"No problem."

After giving his credit card information, James left his car keys in the center console and hiked home.

———

Twenty minutes later, James stepped into his kitchen. Rachel's phone was already connected to the charger on the counter. James connected his phone too. Several years ago, James had suggested leaving their phones downstairs at night. He had been having trouble sleeping, as he had developed a mild addiction to his phone. With his phone near their bed, he had a habit of checking his texts and emails before bed. The wrong message could easily ruin a good night's sleep.

With his phone out of sight, it was also out of mind. Therefore, he never felt the need to check his messages before bed. Rachel had a similar issue and didn't want to be controlled by her phone, so she charged her phone downstairs too.

James went upstairs to their master bedroom. Rachel was already in her pajamas, brushing her hair in the mirror over her dresser.

"You could've waited for me," James said, glowering at her in the mirror.

"I didn't know how long it would take," Rachel replied, her focus on her hair.

James went to the bathroom, brushed his teeth, and changed into his pajamas, which were an old pair of sweatpants and a t-shirt. Rachel was now on her side of the bed reading something on her Kindle, probably some erotic romance.

James snatched his pillow off the bed. "I don't know what's going on between us, but I'm tired of trying and receiving nothing in return. I'm sleeping in the other room."

Rachel didn't reply.

James walked down the hall to one of the guest rooms, thinking that she obviously didn't care where he slept.

EIGHT
HOT PROWL

LOW VOICES WOKE James from his slumber. James sat up and blinked several times, sure the voices were in his dream. He glanced at the clock on his bedside table—*2:08 a.m.* He heard the voices again. It sounded like they came from the vent next to his bed. He rolled out of bed and knelt next to the vent, which was connected to a heating duct that snaked downstairs. The voices sounded muffled and unintelligible, but they were likely male and distinct from each other.

James scanned the room in a panic, unsure of what to do, his heart pounding in his chest. The steep gable roofline of his Cape Cod house created a short, cramped area near the outer walls. Instead of this area being unusable, a storage area or crawl space had been built that spanned the outer walls of the bedrooms.

Heavy steps came from downstairs. The second step creaked, sending a jolt of adrenaline through James's body. James opened the two-by-two door to the crawl space and climbed inside. He shut the door behind him. In the dark space, he realized his mistake. He should've gone to Rachel immediately. Then they could've hidden in the crawl space together. If he tried to go to her now the men would certainly see him, but he could still access her room through the crawl space.

So James crawled in the pitch dark toward Rachel. The guest bedroom he had come from was at one end of the house, and the master bedroom was at the opposite end, roughly one hundred feet away.

The crawl space smelled musty. He felt the rough wood under his hands and knees. Cobwebs broke and intertwined with his hair. His chest felt tight, his breathing elevated. He felt his way past a few boxes, but most of the crawl space was unused. He brushed up against the insulation attached to the wall cavities. The fiberglass caused his arm to itch. He spotted a small sliver of dim moonlight up ahead. He crawled as quickly as possible, careful not to make too much noise.

The sliver of moonlight came from the crawl space door in the master bedroom. The sliver of light brightened. Someone must've turned on the overhead light. He reached for the little knob on the crawl-space door. Then Rachel shrieked, followed by a heavy *thump*. James imagined Rachel being yanked from her bed and dumped on the floor.

"What the hell are you doing?" Rachel asked, her tone authoritative.

James's hand trembled, still touching the crawl space doorknob. He tried to control his heavy breathing. All he had to do was open that door and help her, but he was frozen in place.

"Shut the fuck up," the first intruder replied, his voice muffled as if he were wearing a mask. "Where's your husband?"

"He's here," Rachel said. "He slept in the guest bedroom. The one closest to the stairs."

"He's not there. Where the fuck is he?"

"This is fucked," the second intruder said, his voice muffled like the first intruder but still distinctly different, deeper, with more bass.

They're here for me. James removed his hand from the crawl-space door and crawled backward. He hid behind a few boxes.

Rachel's voice quivered with fear. "He has to be here. He wouldn't leave me." Then Rachel said something inaudible.

"Search the fucking house from top to bottom," the first intruder said. "Start with the guest room by the stairs. *Find* him."

"You find him. It's not my fucking job," the second intruder replied.

The first intruder was quiet for an instant, then said, "Stay with her."

Heavy footsteps left the master bedroom, presumably the first intruder going to search the house. Rachel and the second intruder didn't talk, which was comforting to James. *They're obviously here for me. She'll be okay*. The crawl-space door from the guest room opened roughly one hundred feet away from James's location. A flashlight illuminated the crawl space. James tucked himself into a ball, ducking his head behind the boxes. He imagined the first intruder crawling through the storage space and finding him. But then the crawl space went dark again.

Several minutes later, the first intruder returned to the master bedroom and said, "He's gone."

"Check in there," the second intruder said.

The first intruder opened the crawl-space door in the master bedroom. James tucked himself into a ball again, making himself small behind the boxes. Ambient light and the direct beam of the flashlight pierced the crawl space. The first intruder was only ten feet away from James, maybe less. James was certain the man could hear his heartbeat and his breathing. But the first intruder flicked off the flashlight and shut the door.

"He's not here. He must've slipped out the back," the first intruder said.

"What do we do now?" the second intruder asked.

"Do your job. I'll watch her."

Heavy steps left the master bedroom. James figured it was the second intruder going to do his job. *What is his job?*

The first intruder and Rachel were likely farther away from James now, or maybe they talked lower, or maybe both because their words were inaudible. James moved out from behind the boxes and put his ear to the crawl-space door. Their conversation was still partially inaudible, but he heard bits and pieces of the conversation.

"Who are you _ _?" Rachel asked. "_ scaring _."

"Shut up," the first intruder replied.

"You _ _ _ tough. I don't _ it."

"I don't give a fuck."

"Stop _ _ at me. What's _ _ you? You're out of _."

"Now _ notice _"

"If you _ me, _ _ do what _ say."

The first intruder raised his voice. "You think I'm stupid, don't you?"

Rachel replied in a soothing voice that was inaudible to James. "_ _ _."

"Bullshit. I know the truth."

"_ _ _."

"Stop *lying*. You're _ _ _."

"_ _ _ what you're talking about."

James thought that if anyone could calm a psychopath, Rachel could.

"Don't *lie*. _ _ me," the first intruder said.

"She doesn't know _ _ _ _. She's _ _."

The master bedroom door shut. They were quiet for a moment, then Rachel said in her authoritative voice, "Don't look at me like that."

"You don't _ _ power _," the first intruder said.

Their footsteps moved closer to the wall. James heard more of their conversation as a result.

"Take off your clothes," the first intruder said.

"Fuck you."

There was a *thud*, followed by a yelp from Rachel.

James grimaced. He wanted to go to Rachel, to fight the intruder, but his fear covered him like a straightjacket. His hands formed into tight fists; his fingernails dug into his palms.

"Fuck you," Rachel said again.

"Do it," the first intruder said.

"Or *what*? You'll kill me? You don't have the balls."

Another *thud* came, followed by several more. Rachel yelped again, then grunted several times.

James's mind was transported back in time, back to his childhood bedroom. He was there and here, a spectator in two places at the same time. Heavy steps climbed the stairs. His stepfather was so drunk he had to rest halfway up, using the handrail for balance. James hid under his covers, hoping he would leave him alone. Sometimes he did. Sometimes he didn't. His bedroom door opened. James tucked himself into the fetal position, covering his head with his hands and making himself small.

"Is that what this is about? You're desperate to fuck me?" Rachel said.

Another *thud* and a groan. Then a struggle, followed by grunting, coming from the first intruder, and skin slapping against skin. Rachel went silent. Labored breathing came from the first intruder.

His stepfather lumbered into his bedroom and yanked the covers off his bed, exposing James. His stepfather grabbed James by his shoulders and flipped him to his back, breathing heavily. James turned his head away from the smell of alcohol.

"Look at me, … you lil' shit," his stepfather slurred.

James kept his head turned and his eyelids sealed shut.

"Look at me!" His stepfather smacked him several times across his face.

James cried and called for his mother.

"Quit your fuckin' cryin'. I barely touched you."

James nearly hyperventilated, with short shallow breaths and tears streaming down his face.

"My trash can fuckin' stinks. It's filled to the fuckin' brim. You know why?"

"I'm sorry. I'm sorry," James said.

James had learned to immediately apologize for his transgressions.

"How many times do I have to tell you … to put out the trash on Friday mornin'? Now we gotta smell garbage for a fuckin' week." His stepfather rolled James to his stomach and punched him several times in the back.

Rachel was dead silent. The slapping of skin ended in a flurry and a long groan. The labored breathing of the first intruder regulated.

Rachel cackled. "Is that it? You fucking loser." Then her laughter ceased, like it had been turned off at a switch. She said, "I'm sorry. Please, don't."

No reply came from the first intruder.

"Please," she said.

"I know who you really are," the first intruder said.

"James! Help me!"

James flinched as two gunshots popped, followed by the smell of sulfur. His entire body trembled. James went back to his childhood bedroom. He remembered his mother standing in the doorway of his room, after the beating. She shut the door without a word.

In the present, the master bedroom door opened and heavy steps ran into the room.

"What the fuck, man? We weren't supposed to hurt her," the second intruder said.

"She attacked me. Tried to take my gun," the first intruder replied.

"Naked?"

"Yeah."

"You're a sick fuck. This is your ass, not mine."

"Did you open the safe?"

"It's open. I'm not dealing with this shit. I'm fucking done."

Two more gunshots popped, startling James again.

The first intruder said, "Now you're done."

NINE
UNTIL DEATH DO US PART

THE HOUSE WAS QUIET, but James still hid in the crawl space, sure that the intruder would return to finish the job.

After what felt like an hour, James emerged from his hiding spot, like a coward. Rachel lay on her side, naked, a hole where her right eye used to be and another hole between her breasts. Her face was ghastly, streaked with blood on her right cheek, her left eye frozen open in terror. Blood pooled around her head and body, staining the oriental rug.

James knelt behind her, his hands trembling. He closed his eyes, the sight of her unbearable. He touched her bare shoulder. She already felt a little colder than usual. He lay behind her, his head on her shoulder, and sobbed. He lay with Rachel, like two spoons for a long time, not wanting to accept *until death do we part*.

He finally lifted his head from her shoulder and retracted his arm, where he'd wrapped her up in a hug, just above her chest wound. He staggered to his feet, the room spinning above him. Rachel's blood stained his pajamas. He gripped the nearby bedframe to stop himself from collapsing.

As his vision cleared and his legs strengthened, he noticed the man lying across the room, near the door. James stepped to him tentatively, half-expecting him to awaken. The man lay on his back, two holes in his chest. He wore black pants, a black hoodie, and a black balaclava that covered his entire face and head, except for his eyes.

James's heart thumped as he reached down, gripped the balaclava, and removed the man's mask. He saw his stepfather's face for a split second, but the man was ultimately unfamiliar. He appeared to be in his thirties or forties. His dark hair was buzzed tight to his scalp. His stubbly beard appeared more lazy than intentional. His cheeks were chubby, matching his dad-bod shape.

James left his master bedroom in a fog. When he entered the kitchen, he couldn't remember descending the stairs. He grabbed his cell phone from the counter, disconnected the charger, and dialed 9-1-1. It was the first time in his life he'd ever dialed the emergency number.

"Nine-one-one, what is your emergency?" a female operator asked.

James hesitated, struggling to find the words.

"Nine-one-one, what is your emergency?"

"I, uh, ... two men broke into my home. Killed my wife."

"Are the men still inside your home?"

"One's dead. The other one left."

"Are you hurt or in danger?"

James was embarrassed to answer, "No."

———

After hanging up with the emergency operator, James stared at Rachel's cell phone sitting on the counter, attached to her charger. He remembered her texting when he had entered her office less than forty-eight hours ago. She had set her phone face down, not wanting him to see the screen. He thought about her lack of interest in sex. Her lack of interest in him. He thought about her smelling like cologne at two in the morning.

The cops will probably take her phone. If she was having an affair, I'd rather know before they do. He unhooked her phone from the charger and pressed the button on the side, waking the cell phone. Unlike James's phone, Rachel's asked for a password. He guessed a few times with birthdates and their anniversary date, but it never opened. He returned the phone to the charger.

James remembered something the first intruder had said to the second. *Did you open the safe?* James went to his office and checked under his desk. The door to his safe had been pried open, revealing an empty safe. Teeth marks from what resembled a crowbar dented the door edge and the locking mechanism.

TEN
THE BOX

DETECTIVE HARVEY BANKS entered the small square room, bringing the smell of cigarettes. A two-way window was on the wall across from James. Cameras pointed at them from the ceiling corners.

Detective Banks set a Styrofoam cup of coffee in front of James. "Here you go, James."

James nodded to the stocky detective and stared at the black coffee.

Banks appeared to be near retirement, with deep furrows across his forehead and a weathered face. He had the face of a serious man with a wide-set nose, deep-set dark eyes, and skin reminiscent of James's coffee.

Detective Banks sat across from James at the metal table, a notepad and a pen before him. Detective Frank Decker sat next to Banks, mean-mugging James. Decker was younger, maybe mid-thirties, tall and athletic, with rugged good looks that were muted by his obvious disgust for James.

"You're telling me you didn't hear anything?" Detective Decker asked.

James raised his bloodshot eyes. "No."

Decker scowled at that. "What made you wake up, if not the gunshots?"

"I don't know."

"The perp or perps might've used a suppressor," Detective Banks said to Decker.

Decker grunted but otherwise ignored Banks. "Were you and your wife having marital difficulties?"

James furrowed his brow. "What does that have to do with anything?"

Detective Banks interjected, "We're sorry to even ask, but any little detail might help us find the killer. The devil's often in the details."

James nodded. "We argued sometimes, but we weren't verbally abusive."

Decker narrowed his eyes. "What about physically abusive? Did you ever hit your wife?"

James glowered at Decker. "*No*. Never."

"I'm sorry, James. We have to ask," Detective Banks said, his teeth tinted yellow.

James sipped his coffee, wondering if their good-cop, bad-cop routine was planned. *Are they interrogating me? Am I a suspect?*

Banks continued. "Do you know of anyone who could've hurt your wife?"

James set his coffee cup on the table, his hands still shaky. "A client maybe. She meets her clients in her home office. Some of them are criminals, referred to her by the state as part of their parole or sentencing."

Banks scribbled some notes. "In order to investigate any of her patients, we would need probable cause. Otherwise, doctor-patient confidentiality applies. Do you have any concrete evidence pointing to a particular patient?"

"Recently she talked about a guy whose first wife died by getting crushed under their car while changing a tire."

"That's suspicious."

"Rachel thought so too. He got a big settlement after her death.

Now he's married to a wealthy older woman. Rachel told me that she was afraid of him." James's voice caught. He cleared his throat, regaining his composure. "Rachel was worried that he might kill his current wife. I asked her why she didn't just drop him as a client and call the police. She told me that she didn't have any concrete evidence to report, and she didn't want to drop him because, if she did, and then he killed his wife, she'd feel responsible."

"Did she give you a name?"

James shook his head. "No."

Detective Decker sat silent, staring at James, his arms crossed over his chest.

"Anybody else you think could've hurt her?" Detective Banks asked. "Anybody who might've had a disagreement with her even?"

James shook his head again. "Everyone loved her."

Decker clenched his jaw.

"Was anything else missing besides your"—Banks flipped his notepad backward until he found it—"coin collection?"

"I don't think so, but I didn't go through the house and really check either."

"Who knew about your coin collection?" Detective Decker asked.

"Rachel, and that's probably it, unless Rachel told people. She might've told her parents, but I never heard her talk about it."

Decker scowled. "Then there's no telling who knew. All it takes is one comment to the wrong person, then some criminal finds out and cases your house. That's why you should keep your valuables in the bank."

James pressed his lips together in a flat line.

"Did you have any rare coins that would be noticeable if they came up for sale at a pawn shop or a coin shop?" Banks asked.

"I had an 1872 Carson City minted Liberty Gold double eagle, graded at MS60. There are only eight in existence with that grade.

It would be noteworthy if it was for sale. It would probably sell for around $60,000."

Banks let out a low whistle. "That's some coin. I have to admit that I know nothing about coins. Could you send me some information about it?"

James nodded.

Detective Banks closed his notepad. "I think that's it for now."

They all stood from the table. Detective Decker left without a word, leaving the door open in his wake.

"I'm assuming you wanna inform Rachel's parents?" Detective Banks asked. "We can do it, but it's usually better coming from a family member."

James slumped his shoulders. "I'll do it."

"Thank you for your cooperation," Detective Banks said, holding out his hand.

James shook his hand.

"I almost forgot." Detective Banks reached into his inside jacket pocket and removed a pamphlet. "This is a support group for victims of violent crime and their loved ones. The woman who runs the group is excellent. It might be worth checking it out." Banks handed the pamphlet to James.

ELEVEN
RATIONAL OR RATIONALIZING

AFTER THE POLICE STATION, James went to Walmart to pick up some clothes and toiletries, as he would not be allowed back into his house, not until the police were finished processing the crime scene.

Around 8:00 a.m., James checked into a Holiday Inn Express, electing to pay for an extra day than to wait until their 3:00 p.m. check in time. It was a standard room, with a king-size bed, beige walls, a flat screen facing the bed, and a desk in the corner.

James dropped his Walmart bags and went to the bathroom. He brushed his teeth, showered, and dressed in boxer briefs and a t-shirt. He thought about calling Rachel's parents, but it was still early for a Sunday, and he didn't need much rationalization to postpone that call.

Instead, he sent an email to Rachel's virtual assistant, Gloria, telling her that her employer was dead and asking her to contact all the current clients. One final task for the courteous and conscientious virtual assistant living in Oklahoma.

After tapping Send, he climbed into bed and closed his eyes, hoping to sleep for a few hours, but he kept replaying the events in his mind. James had a knack for auditory learning and memorization, which had helped him ace his SATs and earn an academic scholarship to Penn. But now it was a curse. His mind added disturbing images to play with the looping soundtrack.

James opened his eyes and sat up. He tossed aside the comforter and went to the desk. He grabbed a pen and some stationary from the desk drawer. Then he transcribed everything he heard, thinking that, once it was on paper, his mind might relax. If he thought about an important task or detail for the next day, his mind would obsess over the task or detail until he wrote it down, insuring he wouldn't forget it. But, once he wrote it down, his mind would relax and he'd fall asleep.

He started from the beginning, taking notes and using dialogue tags like a novel. He categorized the home invaders as the Live Man and the Dead Man.

Voices downstairs. Two men. Their words muffled from their masks.

A *thud* came from the master bedroom. Probably Rachel being dragged from the bed.

Then Rachel said, "What the hell are you doing?" Her tone was authoritative.

The Live Man said, "Shut the fuck up. Where's your husband?"

Rachel said, "He's here. He slept in the guest bedroom."

The Live Man said, "He's not there. Where the fuck is he?"

The Dead Man said, "This is fucked." The Dead Man's voice was a little deeper than the Live Man.

James continued to recreate on paper what he had heard. Large chunks of the conversation between Rachel and the Live Man were inaudible, so he used dashes to denote the possible missing words, like a twisted game of Mad Libs or Hangman. When James was finished, he had filled ten pages of stationery.

James read through the written recreation, making edits here and there, doubtful that his memory was perfect. He thought about coming clean with the police, admitting that he hid while Rachel was raped and murdered. That way he could tell them what he had heard. Bile crept up his throat at the very thought of admitting the truth.

If he did admit the truth, it wouldn't take long for the entire town to know he was a coward. But, without all the information, the police were at a serious disadvantage. On the other hand, what did James have? He didn't see the killer. He *might* be able to pick out his voice from a lineup, but, even if he did, that wouldn't be enough for a conviction beyond a reasonable doubt.

James often told his students that human beings weren't rational creatures; they're *rationalizing* creatures. It was much easier to rationalize than to tell the truth. It was much easier for James to convince himself that keeping his secret was the best course of action.

Based on what James had heard, he might've been the target, not Rachel. *They were looking for me. They stole* my *coin collection. The Dead Man said, 'We weren't supposed to hurt her.' The question isn't who would want to kill Rachel but who would want to kill* me. James put his elbows on the desk, holding his head in his hands. *Just because the Dead Man thought they weren't supposed to hurt Rachel doesn't mean Rachel wasn't a target. Maybe we were both targets but the Dead Man thought otherwise or was wrong somehow. Criminals are notorious for low IQs and lies.*

I doubt this was a random burglary. They must've known us somehow. They found my safe. Like Decker said, Rachel could've told anyone. That person could've told someone else. And that person could've told someone else. Gossip travels in a small town. But who? Who would want to kill me?

The first name that popped into James's head was Matt Taylor.

James leaned back in the desk chair and immediately dismissed it. *He's an asshole, but he wouldn't rape his twin sister.* James rubbed the back of his stiff neck, thinking. *What if he's involved in another way? What if he hired the guys? What if they fucked it up? Criminals aren't the most reliable employees. But, even at his worst, Matt wouldn't kill me or even hire someone to kill me. That's insane.*

James rubbed his irritated eyes. His vision was blurry. He only had three hours of sleep before the home invasion, and he was fading fast. He swiveled in his chair toward the king-size bed. Then he remembered his promises to Officer Banks. He did the easy task first. James browsed on his cell phone and found the coin on the biggest online bullion retailer: the 1872 Carson City minted Liberty Gold double eagle. It wasn't exactly his coin, as the grade was AU58, one grade lower than the MS60 of the coin James had, but all the other specs were the same. James emailed the link to Detective Banks, advising him of the grade difference.

Then James scrolled through his contacts to Linda Taylor. He imagined Linda being hysterical when James broke the news. He checked the time on his phone. It was almost 10:00 a.m. *Still early for a Sunday.* They might be at church. James went to the bed, set his phone on the bedside table, and crawled under the comforter. He no longer heard the voices. They had been banished to Holiday Inn stationery.

Now he saw Rachel. Snapshots in time. Her mischievous smile, just before she shared something funny. The way she gazed at James on their wedding day, as she said her vows. The subtle curve of her hips. The way her chest reddened when she was embarrassed. James couldn't turn it off. He sobbed with the realization that these memories were all he had left of her, and they would eventually fade to nothingness.

TWELVE
GUILT

RACHEL KNELT on their oriental rug, naked, her trembling hands held up. The masked man aimed a handgun at her. James stood next to the man, seemingly invisible to him but not to Rachel.

She gaped at James with glassy eyes. "James. Help me. I'm right here. Please, James. Please help me."

James tried to move, but his body didn't react. The masked man fired his gun, the loud *pop* causing James to jolt upright. He sat in bed, breathless, scanning the hotel room in a panic, searching for Rachel and the gunman. Sunlight filtered into the room from the corners of the curtains.

Then it all came back to him. The rape and murder. His cowardice. He tried to go back to sleep, to think about nothing, to picture black nothingness. He tossed and turned on the edge of sleep, but never succeeding. His chiming cell phone finally killed whatever hope he had of falling back to sleep.

He glanced at his phone on the bedside table. It was Linda. His stomach churned. *She knows*. He grabbed his phone, swiped right, and said, "Hello?"

"James, this is Linda," she said, her voice wavering. "What the *hell* happened? I had to find out from a police officer at church that Rachel was murdered. I can't believe this is happening." Linda took short shallow breaths and cried into the phone.

"I'm so sorry, Linda. I meant to call you this morning, but I fell asleep."

Her words were constricted by emotions. "How can you possibly … sleep … at a time like *this*?"

"I, uh, … I don't know."

Her crying stopped after a long minute. She sniffled and said, "I heard she was *shot,* and you claim to have heard *nothing.*"

James swallowed the lump in his throat. "I … I'm sorry."

"Sorry for *what*?"

"I don't know."

She sniffled again. "I don't understand. How can you be … alive, without a scratch apparently, and my daughter's dead?" She broke down in tears again.

"I don't know. I'm so sorry. I'm so sorry."

Linda disconnected the call.

THIRTEEN
THE PUZZLE

AFTER SLEEPING late into the afternoon, James ate in a nearby diner alone. He returned to his hotel room and tried to sleep again, but his mind was too active. He lay in bed, replaying the events over and over in his mind, trying to understand what had happened.

Finally, James threw off the comforter and went to the desk. He turned on the lamp, sat, and flipped through his recreation of the home invasion, written on ten pieces of Holiday Inn stationery. He read through the notes and dialogue over and over again, trying to put the pieces together.

James still thought he was the target, but he had other questions. He had this nagging suspicion that Rachel knew the men, or at least one of them, the one she had been talking to. *The Live Man. It had been his job to find me. The Dead Man made that clear when he had said, 'You find him. It's not my fucking job.'*

The Live Man didn't try that hard to find me. Maybe he didn't want to kill me. He didn't seem that upset about not finding me. After looking for like fifteen minutes, he came back and said, 'He's not here. He must've slipped out the back.'

James ran his hand over his face and exhaled. He spoke aloud now, just above a whisper. "It doesn't make any sense. Maybe

Rachel was the target but only for the Live Man, not the Dead Man. Maybe the Live Man double-crossed the Dead Man." James frowned to himself. "He obviously double-crossed him. He's dead. But the rape doesn't make sense. Unless it was personal."

James reviewed the conversation between the Live Man and Rachel that he had heard in bits and pieces. He filled in the blanks, guessing at what was said, underlining the added words.

"Who are you <u>right now</u>?" Rachel asked. "<u>You're</u> scaring <u>me.</u>"

"Shut up," the Live Man replied.

"You <u>must think you're</u> tough. I don't <u>believe</u> it."

"I don't give a fuck."

"Stop <u>pointing that</u> at me. What's <u>wrong with</u> you? You're out of <u>control</u>."

"Now <u>you</u> notice <u>me</u>," the Live Man replied.

James sat up straight in the chair. *Now you notice me. This wasn't just someone Rachel knew but someone who desperately wanted her attention.* James leaned forward, reading the next line and filling in the blanks.

"If you <u>kill</u> me, <u>I can't</u> do what <u>you</u> say," Rachel said.

The Live Man raised his voice. "You think I'm stupid, don't you?"

James didn't feel confident that he had gotten this right. James talked to himself. "Why would the guy get so angry here? All Rachel said was, 'If you kill me, I can't do what you say.'" James tried to remember Rachel's tone. *Was it condescending? Maybe.*

But, after that, Rachel's tone had been much more soothing. *Maybe Rachel thought he was about to shoot her.*

Rachel's soothing reply had been inaudible at the time, so James tried to fill in the blanks, using the context of the situation. "<u>No, I don't</u>." Or maybe she said, "<u>Of</u> course <u>not</u>."

"Bullshit. I know the truth," the Live Man said.

"<u>No, you don't</u>."

"Stop *lying*. You're <u>a fucking liar</u>."

"<u>I don't know</u> what you're talking about."

"Don't *lie*. <u>She told</u> me," the Live Man said.

"She doesn't know what she's talking about. She's a liar," Rachel replied.

James thought, *She doesn't know. Who is* she? *It must be someone who knows Rachel and this piece of shit.* James went back to his papers, reading the next line of his notes.

The bedroom door shut. They were quiet for a while, then Rachel said, "Don't look at me like that."

"You don't have the power anymore," the Live Man replied.

Anymore, James thought. *If I'm right about the word, that implies Rachel had power over him in the past. If that's the case, it had to be a client who was fixated on her. Obsessed with her. Maybe that's why the Live Man wanted to kill me. To get me out of the picture. But then why did he kill Rachel? Maybe he expected Rachel to be happy that he was there to kill me. The guy is obviously deranged. There may not be a logical reason.*

James leaned back in the desk chair and rubbed his eyes. He glanced at the clock on the bedside table—*2:13 a.m.* James stood from the desk and stretched his arms over his head. He had been replaying the events in his head and on paper for nearly six hours straight. He went to the bathroom, brushed his teeth, and went to bed. He thought about watching television, but his eyes were tired, and he didn't want to accidentally see any news coverage. He didn't need to be reminded. He knew better than anyone what had happened. Well, anyone except for the Live Man.

Instead, he turned off the lights and wrapped the sheet and comforter around him like a cocoon.

———

The masked man aimed his gun at Rachel. James stood with him while Rachel was on her knees, naked, begging. "Please, James. Help me. Please, don't leave me."

The masked man turned his head and glowered at James with eyes as black as coal. He didn't say a word, but James knew what he was asking. *Are you gonna stop me or not?*

"Please don't leave me, James," Rachel said, tears streaming down her face.

James pivoted and walked away, down the hallway toward the stairs. The two gunshots jolted James from his nightmare, causing him to cry out, "No! Don't!"

As the nightmare receded, James heard his chiming cell phone on the bedside table. He glanced at the local number and realized it was likely from the college. Then he noticed the time—*9:12 a.m. Shit. What day is it?*

James grabbed his phone and swiped right. "Hello?"

"James? This is Dean Garland."

James sat up in bed, realizing it was Monday. "I'm so sorry, Dean. I know I'm late for class. I'll be there for my afternoon class."

"I don't think that's a good idea, James. I'm so sorry for your loss. I don't want you to worry about your classes. I've already assigned a TA to handle your classes until the end of the semester. I want you to take the next three weeks and the summer to do whatever it is you need to do for yourself and your family."

FOURTEEN
THE OTHER MAN

LATER THAT MONDAY AFTERNOON, James ate a turkey sub from Subway and watched television in his hotel room. James's house appeared on the local news, crawling with police officers and a traffic jam of police vehicles in the driveway.

The anchor said, "A home invasion in Cleona left two dead—"

James hit the Power button on the remote, vanquishing the news. He stared at his half-eaten sandwich, suddenly disgusted by the lunch meat. He wrapped it up in the wax paper and placed it inside the little hotel fridge.

His cell phone chimed.

"Hello?" James asked tentatively, worried that it was another reporter.

"James Harris?" the woman asked.

"Yes?"

"This is Lori Watson from the *Lebanon Chronicle*—"

James disconnected the call. It had been the fifth call from a journalist that day. James powered off his phone, not wanting to engage, especially worried that they might figure out what he did, or, more accurately, what he *didn't* do. He had only kept his cell phone on for the police, but he hadn't heard from them since his interview yesterday morning.

James went back to bed, pulling the comforter over his head. He tossed and turned for a few hours. He finally drifted off to sleep, only to be immediately jarred from his slumber by the pounding on his door. He shot upright, his body buzzing with adrenaline. Someone pounded on the door again, causing James to flinch. He glanced at the clock on the bedside table—*5:48 p.m.*

He slipped out of bed and crept to the hotel room door. James peered into the peephole. It was Detective Banks and Detective Decker.

James opened the door, wearing sweatpants and a t-shirt, his feet bare. "Detectives."

Decker scowled at James.

Banks said, "We have some information we wanted to share with you, and we had a few questions. Can we come in?"

James flipped on the overhead light and moved aside, letting the officers into his room.

"Why aren't you answering your phone?" Decker asked as he stepped into the room.

"Reporters have been calling," James replied.

They congregated in the open area by the television.

"What's this new information?" James asked.

Banks opened a manila folder, retrieved a mugshot, and handed it to James. "You recognize this guy?"

James inspected the image. The man had a chubby face and dark hair buzzed tight to his scalp. "This is the dead guy who was in my house."

"Have you ever seen him before the other night?"

"No."

"His name's Quentin Henderson. Does that name ring a bell?"

James shook his head. "I've never heard of him before."

Banks held up one hand. "Hold on. Think about it for a minute."

James inspected the image again. "I'm sorry. I've never seen or heard of him before the other night."

"He worked for a local locksmith. Did you or your wife hire a locksmith recently?"

"No. Sorry."

FIFTEEN
THE FUNERAL

THE CHURCH WAS PACKED, the pews filled, with people standing in the back. Sunlight filtered through the stained-glass windows. Romanesque columns decorated the corners. James trudged down the center aisle like a bride wearing black, his head down, his eyes furtive. People on both sides gawked at him from their pews, judging his sins. James thought it was likely that the Taylor family had shared their theories about James's cowardice and even culpability for Rachel's death. In the small town of Cleona, it wouldn't take long for the gossip to spread and morph into the darkest and most salacious version of the original.

James didn't make eye contact with anyone until he arrived at the front row, the row reserved for family and a few close family friends. He looked right and left, scanning the front-row pews. Linda and George sat near the aisle on the right, followed by Matt, Michelle, and their two boys. Rachel's grandparents completed the pew.

Matt glared at James.

James turned to the front pew to the left of the aisle. It was mostly occupied by Rachel's uncles, aunts, and cousins. None of them made any effort to make room for James. It reminded James of his wedding day. They'd had the ceremony at a nondenominational church, similar to the one he now stood in. Like then, the majority of the attendees were Rachel's friends and family. James never had many friends, and the ones he did have disappeared after years of neglect. The friends he had since meeting Rachel were actually Rachel's friends first and foremost, such as Liv.

When he had received a scholarship to Penn, James had vowed never to return home. Consequently, he didn't have family at his wedding either. It was a promise he had kept until several years *after* his wedding. Rachel had suggested that James reconnect with his family. James had done exactly that, visiting during holidays and birthdays, but it had ultimately fizzled after James had given his mother $30,000 for his stepfather's cancer treatments. Subsequently, his stepbrother had mentioned *Dad's new Harley* and James knew he'd been taken. James had vowed, *never again*.

As James stood in the aisle, feeling more and more self-conscious by the second, a hand waved him over. James walked to the end of the row. Liv smiled and scooched in, patting the space next to her. James squeezed into the pew and nodded to Liv.

She squeezed his hand and whispered, "You okay?"

James nodded again.

She let go of his hand. "I'm here for you, if you need anything."

"Thanks," James whispered back.

Linda had insisted on planning the funeral. James had written the check to the funeral home and the nondenominational Christian church. The Taylors had taken his money but not his input, not that James had offered any.

The back of James's neck burned from the gawking funeral audience. He turned to confirm his suspicion—that they were all staring at him. Those with enough decency looked away. James spotted a few familiar faces. Damon sat two rows behind James, although he wasn't one of the gawkers. Detective Decker and Detective Banks sat a few rows farther back. They were both eyeballing James, and neither of them had the decency to look away.

James faced forward again. He wondered if the detectives were there specifically to observe him. See how he acted at the funeral. Was he showing the appropriate amount of grief? Was it genuine?

The funeral began, and the pastor spoke in platitudes about life and death. James barely heard a word, lost in his own nightmare, replaying the home invasion over and over again.

Linda Taylor replaced the pastor at the podium. James focused on his mother-in-law. James had thought he should give the eulogy, but Linda had been adamant, and James had figured correctly that he'd be speaking to a hostile audience. Linda adjusted the microphone down and placed a single sheet of paper on the podium. Even in heels she was under five six, and, even with heavy makeup, her eyes were puffy and red rimmed.

"I've heard that losing a child is the greatest pain a person can experience." Linda sniffled. "I can now confirm that to be true." She took a deep breath. "In my heart, Rachel will always be my baby girl. She was two minutes younger than her twin brother. I don't know why anyone would want to hurt someone as wonderful as Rachel. She was a brilliant woman. Very dedicated to her patients. She was everything I ever wanted in a daughter."

Linda dabbed at the corners of her eyes with a balled-up tissue.

More than a few people in the audience cried into their tissues and handkerchiefs.

"I always knew she would be successful," Linda said. "She was successful at everything. I don't think she ever got anything less than an *A* in school, and she went to school for a *long* time, with college and medical school. She was the Homecoming Queen. The Prom Queen. The head cheerleader. She was voted most beautiful and most likely to succeed by her high school classmates.

"She was so ... *special*." Linda dabbed her eyes again. "She volunteered as a counselor for a suicide hotline. She counseled violent offenders, believing that everyone deserved a second chance at redemption." Linda's voice wavered when she said *redemption*. "The fact that this church is packed with people who loved her says a lot about who she was. I miss her terribly." Linda let out a sob and bowed her head.

More people in the audience joined in the display of emotions, but James's eyes were dry, no doubt further fueling his bad reputation.

After a long moment, Linda raised her gaze, her face wet with tears. "Thank you so much for coming. It warms my heart to see so many people who loved my baby girl."

———

James followed behind the casket as the pallbearers carried Rachel out of the church. James was supposed to be a pallbearer, but several relatives jumped in at the opportune time, and no one said otherwise.

Once outside, the Taylor men slid the casket into the back of the hearse. A lazy breeze kept the crowd comfortable, despite the sun and their black clothing. Most of the funeral goers followed the hearse on foot, as the cemetery plot was within walking distance of the church.

James spotted Damon walking away from the crowd and followed. He caught Damon near the back of the church parking lot, next to his old pickup truck.

"Damon," James called out.

Damon turned to James. "Yes?"

James stepped closer. "Not sure if you remember me. I'm James Harris, Rachel's husband."

Damon squinted at James. "I remember you. I just saw you."

"Right. Last Saturday at Matt's house." James paused for a beat, then said, "I was wondering if I could ask you a few questions?"

"About what?"

James glanced over his shoulder. A few funeral goers walked to their cars, but they were out of earshot. "About Rachel."

Damon hesitated, then said, "Okay."

"Do you know anyone who wanted to hurt her? Anyone who disliked her?"

"No. Everyone loved her."

"What about you?"

"What about me?"

"Did you love her?"

Damon blushed. "I knew her my whole life. I always liked her."

James figured he loved her, given his blush, so he changed the subject, electing not to embarrass the little man further. "You ever have any trouble with Matt?"

Damon shook his head, not making eye contact.

"*Never*? You've been working for Taylor Construction for a long time. You've never had *any* issues with him?"

"He can be an asshole sometimes, but that's just him being the boss."

James nodded. "What does he do exactly that makes him an asshole?"

"It's not all the time."

"I understand that."

Damon checked the parking lot, confirming they were alone. "He can be demanding. Expects us out in the field to work like machines."

"Has he been more demanding lately?"

Damon thought for a few seconds. "Probably. Seems more stressed out too."

"What do you think he was stressed out about?"

Damon shrugged. "Not sure. Maybe money problems."

James furrowed his brow. "Money problems? Why would you say that?"

"We have some old trucks that need replacing, but they've

been putting it off. Also, a few months ago, my paycheck bounced. A bunch of other guys too."

"They didn't have enough money to pay you?" James asked.

"Matt said it was a bank error or something. He reissued the checks, and we all got our money, but that never happened when George was running things."

James nodded again.

"Is that it?" Damon opened the driver's side door to his truck, the hinge creaking.

"One last thing. Did Rachel ever talk to you about a coin collection?"

Damon cocked his head. "A coin collection?"

"Yes. A coin collection."

Damon shook his head again. "We didn't talk that much, and she definitely never mentioned anything about a coin collection. Did she collect coins?"

SIXTEEN
THE WAKE

JAMES PARKED down the street from Matt's McMansion. James had picked up his Honda Accord from Scott's Transmission Center the day before. He could've driven Rachel's Mercedes, but he was more comfortable with his car, like a well-worn t-shirt. He wasn't late for the wake, but cars, trucks, and SUVs already lined the nearby streets. James walked to the brick-faced six-bedroom home. George and Linda had wanted to host the wake, but their house was too small.

He entered through the front door without knocking. Black-clad guests loitered with beers, wine, and sodas in hand. A buffet was set up on the kitchen island, featuring Italian food from Sal's. George had insisted on paying for the catering. James made a loop around the first floor, hoping to be seen by the Taylors and hoping to make a quick exit.

James found George and Linda in the living room. They were busy talking, so he didn't interrupt. Guests gawked at James with equal parts curiosity and equal parts disdain. He ambled through the solarium and outside to the deck for a respite. He found Matt filling the coolers with ice.

Matt slammed shut a cooler and said, "Didn't see you at the burial."

"I wasn't there," James replied, annoyed that Matt was keeping tabs on his whereabouts.

"What were you doing? Hiding?"

James clenched his jaw. "I was talking to Damon."

"Damon?" Matt crossed his arms over his barrel chest. "What the hell for?"

"I thought he might have some insight into who might've killed Rachel."

"Why would he have insight?"

"He's known Rachel his whole life, and he's been working for your company since he was eighteen."

"He's a fucking idiot."

"He said you bounced his paycheck a few months back."

Matt dropped his arms to his sides and clenched his fists. "What the fuck's that got to do with anything?"

James squinted at Matt. "Are you having money problems?"

"Motherfucker." Matt stepped closer.

James could smell the beer on his breath.

"What the fuck are you trying to say?"

James stepped back, showing his palms. "I'm just trying to understand what happened to Rachel."

The door from the solarium opened, and Liv joined them on the deck.

"You should know better than anyone. You were there," Matt said, ignoring Liv.

"I was asleep," James replied, also ignoring Liv.

Matt lifted one side of his mouth in contempt. "*Right*. Four gunshots and you didn't hear shit."

Liv moved between the two men, glaring at Matt. "We're all grieving. Don't take it out on James."

"Stay out of it, Liv," Matt replied.

"It's fine." James left the deck, returning to the solarium. Then he made a beeline for the front door, leaving the wake without a single goodbye.

Quick steps followed him outside.

"James," Liv called out.

James stopped and pivoted at the bottom of Matt and Michelle's driveway.

Liv closed the distance between them and said, "Don't go."

James shook his head. "I can't be here."

"You want company?"

"I wouldn't be good company right now."

SEVENTEEN
GOOD FRIDAY

THE NEXT MORNING James lay in bed, staring at the ceiling fan, listening to the rain. The rotation of the fan and the *whoosh* of the rain nearly hypnotized him. Even though it was past 9:00 a.m., the room was dim, the sun hidden behind dark clouds.

James had been allowed back in his house, as the police had finished processing the crime scene, but he was sleeping in one of the guest bedrooms.

His cell phone chimed on the bedside table, waking him from his trance. He sat upright, grabbed his phone, and swiped right. He immediately regretted his decision, thinking it might be the press. It was worse. Much worse.

"Hello?" James said.

"It's your mom," Donna replied. "I know we haven't talked in a long time."

James's voice was hard. "What do you want?"

"I heard about Rachel. I'm so sorry, honey."

"What do you want?"

"Nothing. I was worried about you. Bill's worried about you too. We just wanted you to know that we're here for you, if you need us."

James stood from his bed, wearing boxer briefs and a t-shirt.

"What would I need from you and Bill? To coerce me out of some more money?"

"It wasn't like that. I tried to tell you, but you wouldn't listen. I did think Bill had cancer, and then when he didn't, he was so happy—"

"That he bought himself a Harley with the money I gave you," James replied, finishing the bullshit excuse he'd heard before. "If that were true, you could've taken back the bike and sent me the money, but you didn't do that, did you?"

"It was a misunderstanding. We can pay you back."

"Then go to Western Union today and wire me thirty grand."

Donna cleared her throat. "We don't have that kind of money on hand. It might take a little time."

"That's what I thought." James paced in the guest room. "It's not even about the money anymore. When I was a kid, I had no say over how I was treated. Bill could get drunk and beat me whenever he felt like it, and there was nothing I could do about it, but I'll be damned if I let that piece of shit take anything from me ever again."

"He's not the same man anymore. He's been sober for the past three years. He loves you like his own flesh and blood."

"Really? Did he ever beat Jared and Colt?" James was referring to his younger stepbrothers. Bill had had them with his first wife, who had been a drug addict and was doing a five-year prison sentence for distribution of narcotics, when Bill and Donna had met.

"Of course not."

James spoke through gritted teeth. "But he had no trouble beating the shit out of me."

Donna's voice was whiny. "You always go there. He was young and dumb. It didn't have anything to do with blood. He was more mature with Jared and Colt. If Jared had been the oldest, I'm sure he would've made the same mistakes with him."

"I don't think so, Donna. Jared and Colt aren't that much

younger than me." They were two and three years younger. "And you're just as bad. *You* let it happen."

She was crying now. "I didn't even know."

"I saw you in my doorway. You *knew*."

"I never saw anything. I swear."

"Bullshit, but, even if you didn't see, I told you about it. Remember that?"

Donna sniffled but didn't reply.

"What did you do when I told you he was beating me?"

Donna didn't reply.

James shouted, "*What did you do*?"

"I didn't do anything."

"*No*. You tried to gaslight me, to convince me that nothing happened. When you couldn't gaslight me, you convinced me that I deserved it, that I needed to behave. Remember? You didn't give a shit about the abuse. You only cared that I kept my mouth shut."

Donna didn't reply.

"After I left for college, I vowed to never come back to that house. If it weren't for Rachel, I never would've talked to you again. Looking back on it now, I was right. You're toxic. Bill's toxic. I hope you both go to hell." James disconnected the call and tossed his phone on the bed.

He dressed, his hands shaky, adrenaline still coursing through his veins. He went to the hall bathroom, peed, and brushed his teeth. As he exited the hall bathroom, he looked left toward the stairs, then right toward the master bedroom.

The door to the master bedroom was shut. He hadn't been in that room since Rachel's murder five days ago. James turned the knob, his palms sweaty. Inside, the bedroom was immaculate. The oriental rug was gone, disposed of, along with Rachel's dried blood. He blinked, remembering Rachel's naked corpse on the carpet. His legs felt weak. He leaned against the doorframe and stared at the little door to the crawl space, remembering what he had heard, remembering how he'd hid, while Rachel had been raped and murdered. Tears welled in his eyes.

He blinked again, now seeing the sanitized room in the present. The crime scene cleaners had erased all evidence of the crimes. Only the smell of industrial-strength cleaners remained. Detective Banks had recommended the cleaning crew. Despite the thoroughness of the cleaning, James shut the door and walked away, not ready to exorcise the demons that remained.

EIGHTEEN
THE DEATH BENEFIT

SINCE HE'D RETURNED HOME two days ago, James had mostly avoided the phone, the television, and the internet. He had distracted himself by gardening and reading nonfiction books on his Kindle, books he'd been meaning to read but hadn't had the time. Despite the distractions, his mind had often returned to Rachel.

When his doorbell chimed, he was reading on the couch in the living room. James crept to the front door, approaching from the side so he might catch a glimpse of the visitor through the sidelight window without being seen himself. It was Liv, holding a covered dish.

She pressed the doorbell again.

James snuck back to the living room, not wanting to talk to Liv. He worried that she'd want to talk about what happened. Also, he sensed that Rachel had been right about Liv's crush on James. He wasn't ready for either of those complications.

She tried the doorbell several more times, while James tried to concentrate on his book, *The Water is Wide* by Pat Conroy. His phone buzzed with a text.

Liv: Are you home? I brought you some food. I also wanted to check on you. Text me back.

James crept to the front door and peered through the sidelight window again. It appeared that Liv was gone. He returned to the couch and his book, but he couldn't concentrate. His mind returned to the scene of the crime. James set his Kindle on the coffee table. In search of another distraction, he went to his office and the pile of mail sitting on his desktop.

Rachel had been in charge of their finances, so she paid all the bills and typically retrieved the mail. James had been collecting the mail sporadically, but he had yet to open a single letter. Yesterday, he had ventured into Rachel's office to retrieve the checkbook and the bills in her metal inbox. There were more bills than he had expected, so he had avoided that reality too. But now he needed a new distraction, and paying bills was better than remembering.

James sat behind his desk and filtered through the mail, throwing away the junk and setting aside the bills. Once he had done that, he checked the bills, quickly realizing that something was seriously wrong. According to their check register, they had a little over ten thousand dollars in their joint bank account, although James's monthly paycheck would be posted soon, adding another five thousand and some change, after his health care and pension deductions. People often assumed he was wealthy, but professors at small colleges were paid about the same as high school teachers.

Their three credit cards totaled over $135,000 in high-interest debt. Rachel had several more credit cards from clothing stores. These cards totaled another $42,000 in high-interest debt. They were behind on most of their utility bills by at least one month, some several months. Rachel's Mercedes payment was two months behind. Their mortgage was late, but at least it wasn't months behind.

James rubbed his temples, his head hurting and feeling nauseated at the same time. His frugality was supposed to save him from exactly this situation. He wondered if, on some level, he knew but hadn't wanted to know. It's not like he was unaware of her constant shopping, but she made more money than him, so who was he to criticize? It was easier to let Rachel handle the finances and to believe they were fine.

He took a deep breath, his stomach settling. *I need to think about this logically.*

James put all the bills that needed to be paid into one pile, and the ones that didn't into another. He wrote checks for the utilities and the mortgage. The rest, he wasn't going to pay. In business terms, it was a strategic default.

After paying the important bills and setting aside the rest, one was left. This bill was current, the premium due in two weeks. He might've forgotten about their life insurance policies, if he wasn't staring at the bill.

James remembered meeting with the insurance agent. He remembered signing the paperwork with Rachel. He remembered the death benefit being $200,000, paid to the surviving spouse. He also remembered the premium being around $400 per month.

Three things surprised James about this life insurance bill. It was the only bill that wasn't past due. The monthly premium was $2,120. And the death benefit was $2,000,000.

NINETEEN
MISSING HER

AFTER DEALING WITH THE BILLS, James poured himself a glass of Johnny Walker Black whiskey. Then another. And another. And another. He staggered around the house, reliving Rachel's rape and murder over and over again.

As afternoon gave way to the night, James became conscious of the fact that someone outside could see him through the windows but *he* couldn't see them. So, James went to the garage and found his old aluminum softball bat. Apart from a kitchen knife, it was the closest thing he had to a weapon.

He struggled up the stairs, carrying his bat in one hand, his whiskey in the other. As he lurched forward, the whiskey sloshed around his glass, dangerously close to the rim. He tried to remember Rachel before. In his mind, her beautiful smile was quickly replaced by her pale lifeless face, her remaining hazel eye frozen.

James went to the master bedroom. He leaned his bat against her dresser, gulped the rest of his whiskey, and set the glass on her dresser top. He grabbed the ornate bottle of perfume, spritzed the air, and inhaled. His mind flooded with memories of her. Holding hands while they hiked. Making love on the weekends. Cuddling on the couch with a big bowl of popcorn and an offbeat comedy.

He walked into her closet. It was packed with designer skirt-suits, dresses, shoes, blouses, pants, and jackets. He ran his hand over her clothes. He put a cashmere sweater to his nose and sniffed, but it didn't smell like her.

He exited her walk-in closet and scanned the bedroom. Her dead body appeared in his mind, with a hole in her head and a hole in her chest. He tried to return to the good times in his mind, but he couldn't recover them. It was as if they had been vanquished by the evil, dubbed over for eternity.

James imagined shooting himself in the head. He imagined fucking it up and being a vegetable for the rest of his life. He wasn't competent with firearms. He'd never even touched a gun. He wasn't a believer, but he wondered if he'd go to hell for not helping Rachel. Yesterday, he had admonished his mother for not protecting him as a child from his stepfather. But he wasn't any better. He had done the same, except Rachel didn't live to shame him for his cowardice.

The doorbell chimed. He staggered downstairs, too drunk to conceal his approach to the front door. It was Liv again, holding a covered dish, wearing a tight skirt and a low-cut blouse.

James opened the door, wearing sweatpants and a holey t-shirt, his eyes bloodshot and his balance wavering.

Liv winced at the sight of him. "Oh, James. What are you doing to yourself?"

"I don't know." James pivoted, stumbled back to the living room, and plopped on the couch.

Liv shut the door and followed him inside. "I made you a lasagna."

James forced a smile. "Thanks, Liv."

"I'm gonna put this in the fridge. I'll be right back."

When Liv returned from the kitchen, James said, "You might be the only person who doesn't think I'm a piece of shit."

Liv sat next to James, the hem of her skirt moving halfway up her thighs. "Nobody thinks that."

James hung his head. "Rachel's family does."

Liv squeezed James's hand for an instant. "They don't. They're just hurting, like you."

James shook his head. "I think the police think I had something to do with it."

"That's ridiculous. What makes you say that?"

"They questioned me like a suspect."

"I'm sure that's just procedure."

"They were staring at me at the funeral."

"That doesn't mean anything."

James gestured to the mostly empty bottle of Johnny Walker Black. "You want something to drink?"

"No. I'm fine." Liv turned on the couch to face James. She wore more makeup than usual. Her breasts were mashed together and lifted by her bra. She chewed on her lower lip, as if thinking about what to do next.

"I should go to bed. Thank you for the lasagna." James started to stand, then sat back down, his world spinning.

Liv leered at him.

"What?" James asked.

She placed her hand on his thigh, leaned over, and kissed him. James was stunned for a beat, then reciprocated. They pulled each other into an embrace, their lips locked. James imagined he was kissing Rachel.

She moved her right hand to James's crotch, squeezing his penis over his sweatpants. James groaned, Rachel's familiar perfume wafting into his nostrils. Then she tugged on the waistband of his sweatpants. James lifted off the couch an inch, allowing her to yank his sweatpants and boxer briefs to midthigh, exposing his erection.

In an instant, her head was in his lap. James groaned, his head lolled backward. He imagined Rachel in his college office, kneeling under his desk, taking him in her mouth.

He was already close. It had been so long. James looked down, expecting to see Rachel's head between his legs. Liv's head bobbing up and down jolted him from his fantasy. Her frameless glasses perched on the end of her nose, dangerously close to falling off.

James grabbed her shoulders and pulled her upright. He pulled up his boxer briefs and pants. He couldn't make eye contact with her. "I'm sorry, Liv. I can't."

"I don't understand," Liv replied, her voice shaky. "All these years. I thought … I thought you liked me."

James forced himself to look at her. "Rachel's only been gone …"

"I'm such an idiot." Liv let out a squeak of a sob. She stood and ran for the door, her heels click-clacking on the hardwood.

"Liv," James called out. "I'm sorry."

TWENTY
PONZI

ON SUNDAY MORNING, James didn't dream about the resurrection of Jesus Christ or even the Easter Bunny. He watched the man in the mask shoot Rachel in the chest, then the head. James watched, frozen, his feet sealed in metaphorical concrete. The masked man pivoted, his handgun aimed at James. The man removed his mask. Matt Taylor grinned then fired.

James woke, thrashing in bed, nearly hyperventilating. He felt his chest, frantically feeling for bloody holes, but he was uninjured. James sat upright and surveyed the guest bedroom. Sunlight filtered through the blinds. The ceiling fan turned overhead, providing a gentle breeze. James went to the window and parted the blinds. His orchard bloomed pink, white, and red. For flowering fruit trees, mid-April was the peak of their beauty. The grass and weeds were dark green and dotted with yellow dandelion flowers.

He grabbed his sweatpants and t-shirt from the floor and dressed. He ambled to the mirror over the dresser. He needed to shave. His eyes were bloodshot, and his wavy hair appeared greasy. He retrieved the pamphlet from the dresser top. It was the pamphlet Detective Banks had given him, after they had interviewed him. Or more accurately, after they had interrogated him.

James read the pamphlet.

Safe Communities is a nonprofit organization located in Lebanon, Pennsylvania dedicated to helping survivors of violent crime and their families. As a community, we're all in this together.

James went to his phone on the bedside table and tapped the web address for Safe Communities. He tapped on the support group schedule. A meeting was scheduled for tomorrow night. James slipped his phone into the front pocket of his sweatpants.

He went to the bathroom, showered, shaved, and brushed his teeth. He still felt disheveled and disoriented, despite his improved appearance. He took a deep breath, staring at himself in the bathroom mirror. *Sometimes you have to fake it until you make it.*

After dressing in canvas pants and a fleece, James made himself a bowl of oatmeal. As he ate breakfast, he couldn't shake the sick feeling in his stomach—a mixture of shame, guilt, and regret. He set down his spoon, unable to eat another bite.

He sipped his coffee, trying to think about something else. His thoughts drifted to the possible culprit or culprits. He thought about what Rachel had said about her client shortly before her murder. *With this guy, I feel like I'm staring into the eyes of the devil.* Of course, Rachel never used names when discussing her clients.

James walked to Rachel's office, taking his coffee with him. Her computer and phone were at the Lebanon Police Department. A metal filing cabinet stood behind her desk. Her patient files weren't accessed by the police because they lacked probable cause to break doctor-patient confidentiality. James tried to open the top drawer, but it was locked. The locking mechanism wasn't impressive. He could've pried it open with a screwdriver, but he figured Rachel kept the key nearby. He checked the top drawer of her desk, finding a key ring with several small keys.

The second key he tried opened the filing cabinet. Inside the top drawer were business documents: incorporation papers, licensure, profit and loss statements, bank statements, and credit card statements.

The second drawer held files in hanging folders, the patient names in alphabetical order. Inside the folders were handwritten notes from Rachel's sessions. Rachel talked about her process, so James knew she took notes during her sessions.

James took a large stack from the front, *A* through *D*. He set aside all the female names, knowing the perpetrator was a man. Then he searched for anyone who Rachel had suspected of violence. This was problematic, as there were too many potential suspects, since many of them were referrals for domestic violence convictions. James rubbed his chin, thinking about the profile. *This isn't someone who's just violent. He's calculating. He's cruel. He's sadistic. He's likely sociopathic. He's probably someone who was obsessed with Rachel.*

James searched for men who Rachel described fitting that profile. He found a few who Rachel identified as being calculating or unsympathetic or sadistic or having an antisocial personality disorder, but none had all or even most of those characteristics.

After many hours of research, James finally hit the jackpot—in the *K*s. Rachel described Philip Kennedy as cold, with difficulty forming attachments. Manipulative and narcissistic, likely sociopathic. She also wrote that Philip had an obvious erection during one of their sessions and that she was considering dropping him as a patient because of his attraction to her.

Inside the folder, a three-page form accompanied Rachel's notes. The standard form provided important information. such as the patient's home address and place of employment. Philip Kennedy lived in Harrisburg and appeared to own his own company—Kennedy Cryptocurrency, Inc.

James took Kennedy's file to his office and opened his laptop. Once the laptop loaded, James searched for Kennedy Cryptocurrency. He clicked on the company website. They advertised the Kennedy Crypto Fund with a 15 percent yield and only a 2 percent management fee. James clicked on the Management tab and found a picture of Philip Kennedy, along with a bio. Philip wore a bow tie and had thinning salt-and-pepper hair, dark eyes, and olive skin. His bio read:

In 2015, Philip Kennedy established Kennedy Cryptocurrency, Inc. after twenty years of experience in financial services. He serves as CEO of Kennedy Cryptocurrency, Inc. and fund manager of the Kennedy Crypto Fund. Prior to Kennedy Cryptocurrency, Mr. Kennedy was a fund manager for Blackstone Inc., the largest private equity firm in the world.

Mr. Kennedy is a graduate of the Massachusetts Institute of Technology, with a bachelor's degree in mathematics and a masters from the Wharton School of the University of Pennsylvania.

James wondered how Kennedy could offer a 15 percent yield on an asset with no earnings. James went back to Google and typed *Philip Kennedy Scam*. He expected to find some disgruntled crypto clients airing their dirty laundry, but he didn't. What he found was far more interesting.

The article was buried on the bottom of the second page of Google results. It was from the *Patriot News*, a Harrisburg area newspaper. The date on the article was May 10, 2014, and the title was "Harrisburg Coin Shop Accused of Fraud."

James scanned the article, his eyes wide. Phillip Kennedy had been the owner and operator of Real Money, a coin shop located in Harrisburg that offered sales as well as vaulted storage of precious metals. As the price of gold and silver declined in the mid-2010s, excessive redemptions from their vaulted storage led to bankruptcy and allegations of theft by storage customers, many of whom never recovered their vaulted gold and silver.

One former vault customer summed it up very well. "He probably spent my money years ago. He files for bankruptcy and we're left holding the bag. It ain't right. He should be in prison."

James clicked the contact page of KennedyCrypto.com. He filled out a request for an investment consultation.

TWENTY-ONE
THE DEATH BENEFIT

AS JAMES ATE his oatmeal on Monday morning, he thought about his life insurance policy. He remembered signing some papers for Rachel a few months ago. She had said it was for the renewal of their life insurance policy, but he was pretty sure she didn't mention the massive benefit increase.

James's cell phone flashed, drawing his attention from his oatmeal. It didn't ring or buzz, as his phone was on silent, but the screen showed someone was calling. He figured it might be a journalist, but he was expecting a call from Philip Kennedy's office, so he answered. "Hello? This is James Harris."

"Hi, Mr. Harris. This is Trish from Kennedy Cryptocurrency."

James had written in his earlier message that he had $500,000 to invest, so he wasn't surprised at Philip Kennedy's nearly instant availability. He set up an appointment to meet with Kennedy tomorrow morning.

After breakfast, James went to his home office, pulled the phone number from the life insurance bill, and called the agent. The receptionist vetted him as a client and transferred him to Bruce Irwin.

"This is James Harris. My wife and I have a life insurance policy with you."

"Hold on a second." Bruce likely pecked at his keyboard. "Yes. James Harris and Rachel Taylor-Harris. I have you right here. What can I do for you?"

James took a deep breath. "Rachel was murdered a week ago. Eight days to be exact."

Bruce hesitated for a beat. "I'm, *uh*, I'm sorry for your loss, Mr. Harris."

"James. Please call me James."

"*Uh*, you're probably wondering about the death benefit." Bruce cleared his throat. "In the case of a nonaccidental and nonnatural death, it's standard procedure for First National Insurance to wait until the police close the case before releasing the benefit."

"What if they never close the case?" James asked.

"First National does their own investigation as well. I've heard of these types of cases settling as quickly as a few months or as long as a few years. In the meantime, I'll need a copy of the death certificate."

TWENTY-TWO
THE NUMBER ONE SUSPECT

HEAVY KNOCKS CAME from the front door, startling James from the book he was reading. He set *The Water is Wide* on the coffee table and crept to the front door. He checked the sidelight windows, not surprised that it was Decker and Banks. The police didn't ring doorbells, and they didn't knock politely.

James opened the door. "Good afternoon, Detectives."

"We have a few questions for you," Detective Banks said. "Would you mind coming down to the station with us? We'll have an officer bring you back."

James frowned. "I'm not doing that. You can ask me here."

"It doesn't look good for you if you're not cooperative," Detective Decker said.

"I don't give a shit what it looks like. You're lucky I even talk to you without an attorney." James had thought about hiring an attorney, but there was no physical evidence that he murdered Rachel and therefore no reason to hire an attorney with money he didn't have.

Decker shook his head, one side of his mouth raised in contempt. "What are we supposed to think about that? We're trying like hell to find the perp, and the husband's acting like a guilty man."

"I'm not playing this game. You can arrest me or leave." James pointed toward their car.

Banks showed his palms. "Now hold on, James. For the record, we don't believe you had anything to do with this, but we need more information from you. Can we come in and talk?"

James exhaled, then moved aside.

They sat around the dining room table for four.

Banks tapped on his phone, then set it on the tabletop. "Is it okay if I record this conversation?"

"Go right ahead," James replied.

"So, how are you holding up?"

"We don't need to do the small talk."

Banks leaned back in his chair, nodding. "Okay. Straight to the point. We can do that."

"Where were you while Rachel was being attacked?" Decker asked.

"I told you. I was in the guest bedroom, asleep," James replied.

Decker arched his eyebrows. "You sure about that?"

James gritted his teeth. "I'm not doing this again. Don't ask me questions you've already asked."

"The crime scene techs found your fingerprints on the inside of the crawl space in the master bedroom."

James's stomach tumbled and his face felt hot, but he tried to maintain his composure. "I was in there a few weeks ago, looking for some old pictures."

"Were you in that crawl space on the night of the attack?" Banks asked.

"No. I wasn't," James replied.

"How often did you hit Rachel?" Decker asked.

James drew back. "*What?*"

Decker glared at James. "You heard me."

"I *never* hit her." James thought about the times they had simulated rape. He had hit her then, but it had been consensual.

"The autopsy showed that Rachel had a bruise on her face."

"She was raped and murdered, asshole."

Decker stood from his chair, standing over James. "You think you can talk to me like that?"

James stood too.

Banks sprung from his seat and stood between them.

"The bruise was *old*," Decker said, spittle coming from his mouth. "Rachel got that bruise *before* her murder."

James stepped back.

"Take it easy, Detective," Banks said to Decker. "Let me handle this."

Decker glared at James one more time, then pivoted and left.

Banks faced James. "Do you know how your wife got that bruise?"

James remembered noticing the bruise. "She walked into a doorframe. She said she was texting and walking."

Banks stared at James with a you-can't-be-serious look. "Texting and walking?"

"I know it sounds ridiculous, but that's what she told me."

"Do you remember when she told you this?"

"I think, the day before she was … murdered."

Banks grabbed his phone from the tabletop. "I think that's all for now."

"Do you have any leads? Any suspects?"

"We're working a few leads. The investigation is still very active." Banks narrowed his dark eyes at James. "We're not ruling out anyone yet."

TWENTY-THREE
SAFE COMMUNITIES SUPPORT GROUP

LATER THAT MONDAY NIGHT, James attended a Safe Communities support group for survivors of violent crime and their families. He sat on a plastic chair in a back room of the Lebanon Public Library. They were arranged in a circle, as the survivors recounted their stories.

"I was a really good basketball player," the young black woman said. "I had offers from Division 1 programs." She stared at the carpet as she talked, wringing her hands in her lap. One of her long legs bounced up and down. "It wasn't like my rapist was hiding in the bushes or some shit. He wasn't wearing a mask. He didn't break into my house. I was the dumbass who went over to his house." She raised her gaze, focusing on the moderator across the circle from her. "He was my coach for like seven years. He was like a father to me. You know?"

The moderator, Anna, nodded.

Many of the women nodded too.

James glanced at Anna, then looked away, feeling guilty for noticing her beauty, especially given the setting. She was athletically built, with straight brown hair parted to the side and a smattering of freckles under her eyes. She reminded James of Danica Patrick, the race car driver.

He fidgeted in his seat, inwardly cringing. Every story involved a man attacking these women. As the only male representative of the group, James felt like he owed everyone an apology for toxic masculinity.

The young woman shook her head, as if trying to shake the memory loose. "I let him do it. I asked him to stop. I said, 'Please stop.' *Please*. Can you fucking believe that? I was so used to listening to my coaches that I couldn't even …" She sniffed and wiped the corners of her eyes. She took a deep breath. "I never told my mom. I did go to the police a few years ago. They said there wasn't enough evidence to prosecute. Said I should've reported it when it happened." She swallowed hard. "I never went to college either. Didn't even graduate from high school. Don't even play basketball anymore." She leaned back in her chair and crossed her arms over her chest. "That's it."

The group applauded.

When the applause died, Anna said, "Thank you so much, Denise." Then the moderator scanned the group. "Does anyone else want to share tonight?"

Anna smiled at James, reading his name tag. "James? Would you like to share?"

The entire group stared at James, no doubt wondering why this man was among them.

James shook his head. "I'm sorry. I'm not …"

"It's okay. There's no requirement to share," Anna replied. "If nobody else wants to share, I would like to close with an announcement. There's a great self-defense class at the YMCA on Tuesdays, Thursdays, and Saturdays. Flyers are on the table, if you're interested in attending. There is a cost to the class. It's ten dollars. If anyone wants to come but doesn't have the money, let me know. I can get you in for free." Anna paused for a beat. "I hope to see you all next Monday. Same time, same place. Thank you all for coming."

Everyone stood from their plastic chairs and ambled toward the door, talking among each other. A few women grabbed flyers from the back table. James followed them toward the exit, stopping at the table. He grabbed a flyer too. It read:

Reggie's Rangers. Learn basic self-defense from a former Army hand-to-hand combat instructor. Learn practical techniques to improve situational awareness and to avoid danger. Learn how to defend yourself in the event of an attack at home or in public.

"Are you thinking of coming to a class?" Anna asked.

James looked up from the flyer. "*Uh*, maybe. I was thinking about it."

"You should come. It's a great class."

"Not sure if I'm free. I'll have to check my schedule."

Anna nodded with a small smirk, as if she knew he was lying. "Well, I hope to see you there."

"Thanks."

Anna collected a few errant disposable cups from their coffee break. They were alone now.

"You need any help?" James asked.

Anna put the cups together, then held them up. "This is it." Then she tossed them in the trash. "So, what did you think of the group?"

James shoved his hands into his pockets. "It was … it was hard to hear their experiences. I felt …"

"Uncomfortable?"

"Yes."

"I imagine it's hard to hear, being the only man."

James nodded. "That's for sure. I kept feeling like I should apologize for my gender."

"There are plenty of terrible women in the world. Doesn't mean I'm responsible for their behavior. You're not responsible for those terrible men either."

"Thanks."

Anna grabbed the remaining flyers from the table. "I hope you'll come back to group next week."

James smiled. "I will."

TWENTY-FOUR
BLACKMAIL

PHILIP KENNEDY'S office was well-appointed, with a massive mahogany desk, a workstation with three computer screens, and a sitting area with a leather couch and a flat-screen television. James sat across from Philip at his desk.

"I don't understand how you can offer a 15 percent yield from assets that have no earnings," James said.

Philip Kennedy leaned forward, resting his elbows on his desktop. He wore a bow tie and a vest. "I use derivatives and a proprietary algorithm to produce profits. In fact, I produce far more than a 15 percent profit. So, even if I have a few bad quarters, my clients will still receive their dividends."

"Sounds like a Ponzi scheme."

Philip scowled at James. "I'm not desperate for deposits. I have plenty of clients. If you're unsure about this investment, you should invest in treasuries with the rest of the risk-averse crowd. Of course, the ten-year is only paying about 1.5 percent."

James leaned back in his chair, steepling his fingers, as if he were truly considering the investment. Then he asked, "Do you know Rachel Taylor-Harris?"

Philip's eyes widened for a split second, then Philip said, "No.

I don't. If you're interested in investing, Trish can help you with a wire transfer. If not, I wish you good luck."

James placed his hands on the armrest. "She was my wife. She was murdered nine days ago. Doctor Taylor-Harris? I know you were a patient."

Philip's body tensed. "I haven't seen her in five years, and that information is supposed to be protected. What the *hell* does this have to do with me?"

"Where were you on Sunday, April 10th at 2:00 a.m.?"

"That's none of your business. I think it's time for you to leave."

"I could report you for running a Ponzi scheme."

"I'm not running a Ponzi scheme."

James smirked and delivered the practiced lie. "I have a friend at the SEC, a law school buddy, who would be happy to verify your claim."

Philip shrugged. "Go right ahead. I'm not breaking the law."

James had anticipated this response too. "Even if you are legit, which I doubt, I bet your crypto customers would love to know what happened with your coin shop. I know I wouldn't invest with someone involved in fraud."

"I settled with all my Real Money customers. I was never indicted."

"You should explain that in a newsletter. The title could be, *I Was Never Indicted*. I'm sure it'll make your investors feel safe and comfortable." James chuckled. "I have all the time in the world to post on your social media pages every single day. I'll start a blog, investigating you and your past businesses. Then, whenever someone searches your business, they'll also find *me*. It's scary what one determined individual can do to a company's reputation."

Philip spoke through gritted teeth. "What the fuck do you want?"

"For starters, I'd like to know where were you on Sunday, April 10th at 2:00 a.m.?"

"I was asleep at home."

"Can anyone corroborate that?"

"I live alone." Philip glowered at James. "Are we done?"

"Do you still collect coins, Mr. Kennedy?"

"No. Digital tokens are far more profitable."

"Did Rachel ever tell you about *my* coin collection?"

Philip scrunched his face. "Why would we talk about *your* coins during *my* therapy session?"

"Maybe you were talking about your collection and she mentioned mine," James replied.

"No. She never mentioned it. Are we done?"

"The same man who murdered Rachel also stole my coin collection."

"I had nothing to do with it." Philip stood from his seat. "This meeting is over."

James stood from his seat too. "I had an 1872 Carson City minted Liberty Gold double eagle, graded at MS60."

Philip raised his eyebrows. "There can't be more than ten of those in existence."

"Eight actually. I imagine whoever stole the coin will likely try to sell it to a shady dealer who will do the deal for cash off the books."

"I imagine they would."

"I imagine someone who used to own a coin shop might still know those dealers."

"I might."

"Would you be willing to tell those dealers that you're looking for the coin and to ask them to find out a little about the seller?" James asked.

Philip narrowed his eyes. "Why would I do that?"

"If I can recover the coin, based on your help, I'll give it to you. And, of course, I won't interfere with your business. In return, I need information about the seller."

Philip stared at James, appraising the situation, then said, "I'll think about it. Leave me your number."

TWENTY-FIVE
THE SEED

JAMES PARKED in the driveway of George and Linda's redbrick rambler. The afternoon sun was high in the sky, partially obscured by fluffy clouds. George's ten-year-old F-150 and Linda's Ford Escape were parked in front of him. The lawn had just been mowed, and the shrubs were clipped in neat little balls. James had thought about calling first, but he wanted to get an instant and more authentic reaction from Rachel's parents.

He exited his vehicle and walked to the front door. James pressed the doorbell.

Linda answered the door, her face a hard mask. "What are you doing here?"

"I need to talk to you and George. It's important," James replied.

She pursed her lips for a moment, then stepped aside. "George is in the basement, working on a model."

In his retirement, George had returned to a hobby from his childhood, building model airplanes.

James followed Linda into the living room.

"Wait here," Linda said. "I'll get George."

The couch was light green, the carpet was shag, and the wallpaper completed the seventies decor. A grandfather clock stood in the corner, a gift from Matt after George had agreed to let him run the company instead of selling it to fund his retirement.

George and Linda appeared in the living room.

"What's this about?" George asked, his posture stiff.

"A few months ago, Matt bounced the paychecks to his employees. I was wondering if you knew anything about that?"

Linda looked at George, her face etched with concern.

George furrowed his brow. "I don't know what you're talkin' about."

"I was wondering if Matt was having money problems?"

George's face reddened. "He's doin' great. The company's doin' great."

"You sure about that? Matt's not the frugal businessman you are."

"How's this any of your business?"

Linda watched George and James argue back and forth, like a spectator at a tennis match.

"Whoever murdered Rachel also stole $500,000 worth of gold and silver from our house," James said. "The safe was hidden. Whoever did it knew Rachel very well."

"What are you sayin'?" George asked.

"There aren't too many people who need money and might know about that safe. Matt is at the top of that very small list."

Linda's face was puckered, like she'd eaten a lemon.

George pointed a shaky finger at James. "You think you can come into my house and accuse my boy of *murderin'* his sister? His own flesh and blood. Where the hell were you? I don't believe for one goddamn minute you were asleep that night. You're either a coward or you had somethin' to do with it."

"I hope Matt didn't have anything to do with it, but, if I were you, I'd check the books at your company." James pivoted and left their house, hoping that the seed he planted would grow.

TWENTY-SIX
GROUND AND POUND

POUNDING CAME from the front door. James set down his spoon and wiped his mouth with his napkin. He figured it was the police again. He rose from the dining room table and went to the front door.

More pounding came from the front door.

James checked the sidelight window, surprised to see Matt on his stoop. James opened the front door. "What are you doing here?"

Matt's eyes were bloodshot. Alcohol emanated from his pores. Matt grabbed James by his collar and dragged him from the doorway, before tossing him off the stoop, into the grass. James tried to rise, but Matt mounted him, punching him in the face, UFC ground-and-pound style. James covered his head with his hands and forearms, but some blows still landed.

Matt finally stood.

James lay on the grass, groaning, his backside wet with dew and his face covered in blood.

Matt spat on James. "You're a fucking coward. I heard about your fingerprints in the crawl space. You were hiding, weren't you?"

James rose to one knee and glared at Matt. "If you were involved, I *will* find out."

"My parents told me what you said."

"It's all true—"

"You *fucking* idiot. My parents don't need to hear that shit from you. I was gonna tell 'em. You fucked that up for me."

"You stole my coins."

Matt ran his hand over his face. "My company's finished. We'll be bankrupt by summer. I'm gonna lose my fucking house. If I had all your money, why am I about to lose everything I got?" Matt paused for a second, waiting for an answer that never came. Then he pointed at James and said, "Stay the fuck away from my family."

TWENTY-SEVEN
THE DEVIL

MATT LEFT, kicking up gravel as he gunned the engine of his pickup. James staggered inside. He went upstairs and checked his face in the mirror. A black eye was already forming. His lip was split, his cheek was bruised, and he had a knuckle-size knot on the side of his skull.

James cleaned his face, his hands shaky. He remembered the last time he'd been punched. The end of August 1999. It had been his last night in Tyrone, Pennsylvania, and his last night in his stepfather's house before traveling to Penn for freshman orientation. He had been at his friend Yusef's house, not exactly celebrating, but reflecting on their past and what was to come. Yusef had an academic scholarship to Stanford. They had been the brainiacs of their little high school, although Yusef was clearly more intelligent.

At the end of the night, Yusef had offered his futon if James wanted to crash, but James worried that his stepfather, Bill, might beat James because he had been out all night without first asking for Bill's permission. So James had gone home. James had tried to sneak through the back door, hoping to avoid Bill, but all the doors had been locked except the kitchen door.

Bill had been waiting for James, sitting at the kitchen table, drinking a Yuengling, a dozen empties on the tabletop. "You think you can come and go like this is a fuckin' hotel?" Bill had asked as soon as James had entered the kitchen.

James had closed his eyes for a moment, trying to hold his tongue. "Sorry. I was at Yusef's house. I lost track of time."

Bill had grunted. "You and that Jew boy."

"I should go to bed." James pivoted.

Bill had raised his voice. "Don't walk away when I'm talkin' to you."

James had faced Bill again.

"You think you're better than me, don't you?"

"I don't—"

"Yeah, you do. With your fancy fuckin' college." Bill had chugged the last of his beer, then crunched the can in his hand. "You think you can make it in the *Ivy League*?" He had said *Ivy League* in a high, mocking voice.

"I think it'll be a lot of work, but I'm used to that."

Bill had scoffed and staggered to his feet. "You don't know shit about real work, *boy*." He had stepped closer to James, within striking distance. "Those *faggoty*-ass professors at Penn don't know shit about real work either. In their ivory towers passin' judgment on *real* men, men like me who work for a livin'. You gonna be one of those limp-wristed professors, or are you gonna be a real man?"

James had been more confident since he had earned his scholarship. The scholarship had represented freedom and power. That had been why he had said, "If my choice is between being like you or some *limp-wristed* professor, I'd choose the professor every day of the week and twice on Sunday."

Bill's punch had landed on James's left cheek, knocking him down for the count. Like all the other times, he had taken his beating without fighting back. He had gone to freshman orientation with a bruised face.

James showered and changed his clothes. His face already swelled from the MMA-style beating Matt had delivered. James returned to the kitchen and retrieved an ice pack from the freezer and an ACE bandage from the junk drawer. He placed the ice pack against his left eye and left cheek. The biting cold was more painful than the injuries. He wrapped the ACE bandage around his head, holding the ice pack in place and covering his left eye.

James replayed Matt's statement in his mind. *If I had all your money, why am I about to lose everything I got?* Despite his justified bias against Matt, James believed Matt was telling the truth. James staggered to Rachel's office, resembling a half mummy. He returned to the files in search of another sociopathic man who was obsessed with Rachel.

―――

After hours of research, he found Nathan Mills. James read Rachel's notes with his mouth ajar.

-Nathan has an antisocial personality disorder, likely sociopathy and narcissism.

-Often plays the victim, regardless of blame and circumstances.

-Has trouble forming attachments.

-Nathan described the accident with his first wife. They had a flat tire. She crawled under their SUV to change the tire and the SUV fell on her, killing her instantly. Why was she crawling under the vehicle to change the tire? Why was she changing the tire to begin with? Nathan prides himself on being an alpha male. Shouldn't he have changed the tire?

-No charges were ever filed against him.

-Nathan's current wife is fourteen years older than him and a wealthy surgeon. Nathan claims to be an independent investor, but he likely lives off his wife.

-Nathan has been cagey about revealing any information that could be relayed to the authorities.

-He leered at me during our session today. His attraction for me is undermining his therapy. Of course, if he has a sociopathic antisocial personality disorder, therapy won't help anyway.

James remembered talking to Rachel about this guy the day before she died. Rachel had described the accident with the SUV falling on the first wife. James thought about what Rachel had said about him.

He said it aloud, "*I feel like I'm staring into the eyes of the devil.*"

James imagined driving to Nathan's house and confronting the psycho. However, it was after midnight, and accosting a sociopath wasn't the smartest idea. He thought about calling Detective Banks. *But what can he do? According to him, Rachel's patient files require probable cause to breach, so these files are useless to the police. Shit. I'm committing a crime by looking at them.*

James took Nathan's file to his office. He sat at his desk and opened his laptop. Once it loaded, he typed Nathan Mills into the Google search bar, but he didn't find any independent investors with doctor wives. His common last name wasn't helpful.

Using Nathan's name and current address, James purchased a background check from PeopleFinder.com. *Jackpot.* Unsurprisingly, Nathan had been arrested before. Several times actually. Fraud a few times, burglary, assault. James found his mugshot, immediately recognizing the man. James had seen Nathan leaving Rachel's back office in his red Corvette, two days before Rachel's murder.

TWENTY-EIGHT
THE BLACK WIDOWER

THE NEXT DAY James drove through an upscale neighborhood of McMansions, many being serviced by lawn and landscaping companies. He parked in front of a stone-faced McMansion with three chimneys and a five-car garage. James exited his Honda. The sun warmed his face. The roar of a zero-turn mower played in the background. James ambled up the paver driveway and the walkway to the front door.

He pressed the doorbell. Chiming sounded inside. James cupped his hands around his face, blocking the sun, and gazed into the door window. The foyer was vast, with massive potted plants and a chandelier.

After waiting a few minutes, James hiked around the house, peeping into the windows where possible. The decor was modern and impractical. Nearly everything was black, white, or silver.

In the rear of the house was an indoor pool, with floor-to-ceiling windows facing the back lawn and the forest beyond. James peered into the window, spotting Nathan lounging on a chaise longue, wearing a white robe.

A young woman dove into the pool. She giggled when she came up for air. She motioned with her finger to Nathan and said, "Get in here."

Nathan stood from the chaise longue with a smirk on his face. He opened his robe, revealing a Speedo bathing suit that left little to the imagination.

The young woman cheered her Adonis.

Nathan strutted toward the pool edge, but something caught his attention. He stared directly at James in the window. Then he ran for the exit, his eyes still on James. Nathan shouted, "Hey. What the fuck?"

James stepped back from the window. His stomach churned. He fought the urge to run, afraid of another beating, yet knowing that this was exactly what he must do.

Nathan exited the back door, wearing nothing but his little black bathing suit. He stalked toward James. Nathan was taller and more muscular than James had remembered, imposing, even with squiggly pubic hairs escaping his banana hammock. "Who the fuck are you?"

"I'm James Harris. My wife was Rachel Taylor-Harris. She was murdered," James said, his voice wavering.

Nathan crossed his arms over his chest. "I heard. What's that got to do with me? And what the hell are you doing, sneaking around my house?"

"You were a patient."

"That's confidential."

"I saw you leaving my house in your Corvette."

"You need to get the fuck off my property before I call the police."

"Where were you on Sunday, April 10th at 2:00 a.m.?"

Nathan crowded James. "That's none of your fucking business. You want another black eye?"

James stepped back, showing his palms, his heart pounding. "I don't think you're involved with Rachel's murder—"

"Damn right, I'm not involved."

"I'm trying to rule everyone out."

Nathan narrowed his eyes. "You trying to rule out *all* her patients or just the ones you think could kill her?"

James deadpanned, "Just the ones *Rachel* thought could kill her."

Nathan cracked his knuckles. "You need to get the fuck off my property."

"If you tell me where you were on April 10th, I won't tell your wife about your little swimming buddy."

Nathan reddened. His neck vein pulsed. "I could beat your ass right here for trespassing." He crowded James again.

James stepped back again, pretty sure Nathan might have touched him with his protruding penis. "Please. I'm just trying to find out what happened to my wife."

Nathan took a deep breath. "What day was that again?"

"Sunday, April 10th at 2:00 a.m."

"That's the weekend before last."

James nodded. "That's correct."

He scrunched his nose in disgust. "I was on vacation with my fat-ass wife."

TWENTY-NINE
ALIBI

JAMES RETURNED HOME and ran a background check on Nathan's wife, Cheryl. Nathan had refused to give James her number, but James found her place of employment on her background check.

After a few phone calls, a vague threat regarding Nathan possibly going to prison, and a long hold, he was on the line with Dr. Cheryl Mills.

"This is Dr. Mills," she said.

"Hello, Dr. Mills," James replied, sitting at his desk. "Thank you for taking my call. My name's James Harris. I'm investigating the murder of your husband's psychologist."

Dr. Mills inhaled sharply. "I, *um*, …"

"The murder took place on Sunday, April 10th at 2:00 a.m. Can you vouch for the whereabouts of your husband during that time?"

She sighed with relief. "We were on vacation in Key West. Our flight left that Sunday morning. I think it was a ten o'clock flight, so he was definitely in Key West at 2:00 a.m. I can provide evidence, if you need it. Are you a police officer? I don't think you mentioned a title."

"I'm Rachel's—the victim's—husband."

"I'm sorry for your loss. I need to get back to work."

"My wife thought your husband killed his first wife. She was worried about you."

"She died in an accident, not that it's any of your business—"

"She thought you were in danger—"

"How could you possibly know any of this? Whatever conversations my husband had with his therapist are privileged."

"I read her notes. Please be careful, Dr. Mills. He's dangerous."

"This is highly inappropriate. My husband's a good man. He has his demons, but that's why he was in therapy. He doesn't need to be judged for it. Do *not* contact me again." Dr. Mills disconnected the call.

James set down his phone with a heavy exhale. He thought Nathan Mills was likely a murderer, but he doubted Nathan was Rachel's murderer. He went back to the patient files, hoping to find another suspect.

———

Six hours later, among the *W*s, James found Damon Williams's file. James scanned his new patient form, confirming it was the same Damon who worked for Taylor Construction. The new patient form was dated March 12, 2018, over four years ago.

James read Rachel's notes:

-Damon has an attachment disorder, stemming from his father's abandonment.

-Damon has extensive trauma from his father's absence and the physical and sexual abuse perpetrated by his mother's various boyfriends. At sixteen years old, Damon went to live with his cousin Liv and her parents until he graduated.

-Damon suffers from loneliness and depression as a result.

-Damon had a crush on me in high school. He may still. I had reservations about taking him as a client, but he has been respectful and conscientious in therapy, thus far.

-I referred Damon to a colleague, as Damon's attraction for me was beginning to interfere with our sessions. He was unhappy with my decision.

James wasn't sure when Rachel had ended her therapy with Damon, as the notes were not dated.

THIRTY
THE REVELATION

JAMES PARKED in a visitor space in the townhouse community. He exited his vehicle. Moths fluttered about the post lights in the parking lot. The moon was nearly full. James walked to a middle unit townhouse and knocked.

Liv answered the door, wearing sweats and a frown.

James had texted earlier and asked her if he could come over and talk.

Liv had replied with an unexcited, *I guess*.

"Hi," James said.

"Hi," Liv replied, guarding the doorway.

"May I come in?"

Liv lifted one shoulder, but she stepped aside. James followed her into the living room. The decor was country, with lots of wood, plaid, dried flowers, and trite knickknacks, with messages in loopy cursive that said things like, *Home is where the heart is*. A mystery novel sat on the end table, next to her recliner. Liv sat on her plaid couch. James sat at the opposite end of the couch.

"I'm really sorry about the other night," James said. "I let it go too far."

"Ya think?" Liv replied, still wearing that frown.

James dipped his head. "I'm sorry. I don't want to lose you as a friend."

Liv pursed her lips. "I don't want that either."

"Thanks, Liv. You've always been there for me."

She forced a smile. "You know me. Miss Reliable."

"You are Miss Reliable. It's a good thing. It's a *rare* thing."

Liv blushed. "Thanks."

"You're welcome." James paused for a beat. "I wanted to ask you a few things about your cousin Damon."

"Okay."

"You said that he was in love with Rachel in high school."

"Head over heels. He would've done anything for her."

"Did they ever go out?"

Liv laughed. "No way. Rachel always went for the top-tier guys."

"Was Damon heartbroken over Rachel?"

Liv shook her head. "I don't think he ever expected her to like him like that. He was in love with her, but it's not like he made a big move."

"A big move?" James asked. "Does that mean he made a small move?"

"The summer before our senior year, he tried to kiss her at a party, but she turned her head and laughed at him."

James winced. "That must've hurt."

"I think he's used to being hurt. He didn't have the best childhood."

James nodded. "You think he's capable of murder?"

Liv drew back. Her voice went up an octave. "*No*. I've never even seen him in a fight. Damon's a little weird, but he's a nice guy. Are you investigating her murder?"

"I'm just trying to understand what happened."

"So am I." Liv took a deep breath. "I think it could've been personal."

"What makes you say that?"

"I loved Rachel. She was my best friend, but she wasn't always good to people."

"What do you mean by that?"

"She could be very … competitive."

This was true. James thought of the summer they started biking the trail in Mount Gretna. It had been his idea to buy the bikes, to do something healthy together. The first time they'd biked together had been fun, until James had raced her near the end of their route. James had beaten Rachel back to the car, although she went a few hundred yards past the car, making sure she had biked farther, if not faster.

The next time they'd biked, and, every time after that, Rachel had been a woman on a mission. No longer did they leisurely pedal through the woods of central Pennsylvania. Rachel had always taken off with a blistering pace that James couldn't match.

The next year, James had taken the bikes to be serviced, and the technician told James that his brakes were rubbing. He'd said, "That'll surely slow you down."

When they returned to the trail, James had no trouble keeping up with Rachel. In fact, he could've easily overtaken her, but James had let her win, figuring that it meant something to her.

"She was a high achiever," James said to Liv. "High achievers are competitive by nature. It's not necessarily a character flaw, although it can rub some people the wrong way."

Liv grabbed a pillow from the couch and crossed her arms over it. "But Rachel took it too far sometimes. She always had to show everyone that she was the best at everything."

"Can you give me an example?"

Liv squeezed her pillow. "There was this guy, Austin. He transferred our senior year. We *never* get transfers, so he was a big deal. He sat next to me in study hall, and we became friends. I had a *huge* crush on him. When he asked me to go to the movies, I was freaking ecstatic. He kissed me after the movies, and I was falling hard for him. We started spending lots of time together, like right away. It was the only time I can remember having a boyfriend while Rachel was single. Usually, it was the other way around. Although, I don't know if Austin ever considered me to be his girlfriend."

James fidgeted in his seat, worried about where this story was going.

"Anyway, Rachel convinced this other girl to have a party at her house while her parents were out of town. Austin and I went to the party. We were drinking and having a good time. Then, out of nowhere, Rachel went right up to Austin and asked him to go upstairs with her. I was speechless. She did it right in front of me and a bunch of other people."

"What did he say?"

Liv shook her head again. "Nothing. He took her hand and went with her."

James cringed.

"I watched them walk up the stairs, holding hands. I was frozen. Then Rachel stopped and told him that she'd never hook up with a loser like him. She said that I was too good for him. Then she kicked him out of the party. It wasn't even her house."

"What happened with you and Austin after that?"

Liv stared at the carpet. "I moved my seat in study hall. We never talked again."

"Shit. That's …"

Liv raised her gaze. "I guess I should've been grateful. Rachel saved me from a douchebag who would've cheated on me, but it all felt so … petty and mean at the time, like she was telling me how she could have any guy, even my boyfriend."

"Rachel's not a cruel person. I'm sure she only did that because she knew what an asshole the guy was."

"I know."

"She should've done it in a better way though."

"Rachel did what she wanted. Ironically, that's why everyone wanted to be her or to be *with* her. It wasn't just her beauty. She had that confidence, you know?"

James nodded. "I know."

Liv's shoulders slumped. "We were like sisters. Closer than sisters, really. She told me everything. We shared our wildest dreams, our deepest secrets." Liv swallowed hard. "I miss her so much."

"Me too."

They sat in silence for a long time.

James finally said, "You remember that story you told me about Rachel getting those guys to jump into the quarry."

Rachel perked up. "That was crazy."

"You said Damon was there."

"Yes. Damon was the first to jump."

"You said the other guys were football players."

"Yes. Tristan Umberger was one of them. He got a scholarship to play football at Penn State. He was a lineman. I think a tackle or something. He played in the NFL for a few years. I don't remember the team though. Last I heard, he lives out in California."

"What about the other guy? The quarterback?"

"Frank Decker. He's a detective with the Lebanon Police Department.

James was speechless, his eyes wide.

"What?" Liv asked.

"I've met him. He's investigating Rachel's …"

Liv broke eye contact. "Oh. I didn't know that."

James was quiet for a moment, thinking about the revelation. "So, Frank Decker was in love with Rachel too?"

"Everyone was."

THIRTY-ONE
THE POST-ABUSE APOLOGY

AFTER THE REVELATION about Detective Decker, James wasn't sure what to do. Decker's high school crush on Rachel didn't necessarily mean anything. On the other hand, James felt that it was at least a conflict of interest. He vowed to bring it up the next time he saw Decker.

Five days later, James still hadn't heard from Detective Decker or Detective Banks. Instead, James listened to a victim of violent crime in the back room of the Lebanon Public Library.

"I'm such a klutz," the middle-aged woman said, sitting among the circle of plastic chairs. "The first time it happened, I spilled my red wine on his shirt at a party. I laughed. I thought he'd laugh too because he knew I was a klutz, but he was really angry. He was really quiet when we left the party. In the car, I asked him what was wrong, and he slapped me. He never even answered me. Just slapped me across the face and drove me home. I cried the whole way there. The next day he was extremely apologetic. Sent me flowers. Begged me to forgive him. It was like the guy who hit me wasn't even him, so I forgave him."

The group focused on the middle-aged woman, nodding along with the parts that resonated with them. Almost all of them resonated with the post-abuse apology.

James wrung his hands in his lap, thinking of his stepfather, although he had never received an apology.

The middle-aged woman took a deep breath. "When we got married, I thought it would stop. I thought he would feel more secure, but it only got worse. He hit me more often. Harder. And eventually it didn't matter what I did, he'd find a reason. I thought he was gonna kill me when I filed for divorce. If it hadn't been for my dad and my brother, he might've. They came with me to the house to get my stuff. My ex was surprised they were there. It was like he thought he had isolated me enough that nobody would help me. It was the first time I ever saw him look intimidated.

"I was only thirty-one when I got divorced, but he had convinced me that I was nothing. So I spent the next two decades repeating the same pattern of dating abusive men until I finally got into therapy." The middle-aged woman scanned the group. "And now … I don't know. I don't know if I'll ever find love. I'm not even looking anymore. I feel like it's a win that I can go home and not worry about being punched in the face." She shrugged. "I guess that's all."

The group applauded.

Anna, the moderator, said, "Thank you so much for sharing, Lois." Anna surveyed the group, her gaze settling on James. "Anyone else want to share? James?"

"No, thank you," James replied.

Some of the women gawked at James's bruised cheek, black eye, and scabbed lip, no doubt wondering about *his* abusive relationship.

"Anyone else?" Anna paused for a few seconds, giving time for a response. "Okay. Let's take a ten-minute break, then we'll talk about de-escalation techniques."

―――

During the break, some went outside to smoke. Others talked in smaller groups, sipping their coffee and eating a homemade cookie. James sipped his coffee by himself.

Anna approached, carrying a napkin wrapped around two chocolate chip cookies. She smiled and held up the cookies. "Want one? They're fantastic."

James smiled back. "Sure."

Anna handed James a cookie and a napkin.

"Thank you." James took a bite of the cookie.

"Pretty great, *huh*?"

James swallowed. "They're excellent."

"Denise made them. She bakes at least as good as she plays basketball."

James nodded. "I'll be sure to thank her."

Anna stared at James's face for a second, then asked, "What happened to you?"

James touched his cheek reflexively. "Oh. Walked into a doorframe. Texting and walking."

"It looks like it hurts."

"I'm fine."

Anna tilted her head. "You sure?"

"I'm sure."

"I missed you at the self-defense class last week. I was hoping you would come."

"Sorry. I was really busy."

Anna grabbed a flyer from the table and handed it to James. "Maybe this week?"

James took the same flyer he'd taken the week before. Class was every Tuesday and Thursday night at 6:00 p.m., and Saturday at 9:00 a.m. at the YMCA.

THIRTY-TWO
REGGIE'S RANGERS

"IT'S ALL ABOUT BOUNDARIES, LADIES," Reggie said.

James stood on the mat, wearing sweatpants and a t-shirt, no shoes or socks. Nine fit women stood around him, also listening to the muscle-bound, bald-headed self-defense instructor. Anna stood next to James wearing yoga pants and a t-shirt, her dark hair in a ponytail. James stole a few glances. Even without makeup, her face was beautiful, with high cheekbones, clear skin, and puffy pink lips.

"Whether it be verbal, physical, or psychological, you have to set boundaries. By setting boundaries, you'll discover the intent of your potential attacker." Reggie paced in front of the group. "We have to be situationally aware. We have to be aware of our surroundings. We have to avoid stupid places and stupid people. What happens if we hang around stupid people in stupid places?"

The group of women said in unison, "We win stupid prizes."

"That's right. Nobody wants a stupid prize. And I better not *ever* see any of you walking around town with your face in your damn phone. Real life ain't in your phone. Y'all need to be real careful about what you're posting on social media too. If I was you, I'd delete all that garbage. You don't need to be on there, broadcasting yourself and your whereabouts to every potential predator in the area." Reggie pointed to a fit woman, wearing yoga pants and a sports bra. "Kate. You got one of those insta-whatever accounts?"

Kate grinned. "Yes."

"How many friends you got on that?"

"Fourteen thousand. But they're called followers, not friends."

Reggie scowled. "Should be called *fools*. You should go right home and delete that account. You don't need fourteen thousand people watching you."

A few women giggled at Reggie's antics.

"All right, let's get loose and get to work. Everyone spread out."

They started with light jogging in a circle around the matted room. After ten quick laps, Reggie called out, "Seven." They proceeded to do seven burpees. A single burpee was a squat, pushup, and jumping in the air all in one long motion. After they did their burpees, they ran around the room again until Reggie called out another number.

Three minutes into the warmup, James was huffing and puffing. He wasn't the only one struggling, but most of the women showed little evidence of fatigue.

Reggie stood over James as he did his burpees. "Let's go, James. Don't give in to the pain. Keep fighting. If you wanna get better, you gotta push yourself."

James swallowed the bile creeping up his throat and finished the warmup … barely.

After the warmup, they paired up and worked on boxing. James wore pads on his hands while Anna hit one hand with a jab, the other with a right cross. She used her hips to generate power. After the one-minute buzzer, they switched places. James tried to mimic Anna's form. For the first twenty seconds, his boxing gloves made a satisfying one-two *pop* against the pads, but his upper body tired quickly thereafter.

"Let's go, James. Get those hands up," Reggie said.

Lactic acid pumped through James's upper body, making his

limbs feel like concrete. At the buzzer, James dropped his arms in relief.

In addition to boxing, they grappled, focusing on breaking common holds used by predators. Anna introduced James to an arm bar. If she hadn't relented, she could've easily broken James's arm. During one of the holds, Anna pushed her backside against James, lifting him onto her back and then flipping him onto the soft mat.

They finished with a common real-world situation.

Reggie motioned with his hand. "Come up here, Anna."

Anna stood next to Reggie in front of the group.

"Let's say you're at the office Christmas party and a drunk coworker is acting a fool. He's had his eyes on you all night. I'm gonna play the drunk coworker. Anna, you play yourself."

They faced each other.

Reggie's words were slurred. "Hey, baby. You wanna go to my place?"

"No. I do not," Anna replied, her words sharp and definitive.

"Come on, baby. You know you want to."

"*No*. Leave me alone."

Reggie glared at Anna. "Don't be a bitch." He reached out and grabbed Anna by the wrist.

Anna took a quick step forward, using her free hand to hold Reggie's shoulder in position. This movement twisted Reggie's arm in a very unnatural position, causing him to let go. Anna then backed away from Reggie in a fighting stance.

James and the rest of the class clapped for Anna.

"That's how it's done, ladies," Reggie said.

THIRTY-THREE
DINNER AT THE DINER

JAMES AND ANNA sat at a corner booth in Mel's Diner, sipping their coffee.

"Tell me the truth," James said. "Are you Wonder Woman?"

Anna rolled her eyes.

"Seriously, you have some fighting skills. Everyone in class did. I felt like a big doofus."

"You weren't a *big* doofus."

"Just a regular doofus?"

Anna smirked. "Not a doofus at all. I thought you did pretty well for your first class. If you keep coming, you'll be a superhero in no time."

"I don't know about that. I've never been much of a fighter."

"You have some athletic ability. I can tell. You were picking up the movements pretty quickly."

"Now I know you're just being nice. I was dying in there. I swallowed my own bile several times."

Anna scrunched her face.

"Reggie was lucky I didn't puke all over his feet."

Anna laughed. "I don't think that would've gone over very well."

James laughed too. "Probably not."

"I hope you'll come on Thursday."

"I think I will."

Anna smiled and took a sip of her coffee.

James smiled and sipped his coffee too.

The waitress appeared with their burgers. James had ordered a side of fries, while Anna had ordered a side salad. They ate in relative silence for a minute. A few elderly men sat at the counter, drinking coffee and eating pie, but the diner was mostly empty. The dinner rush had cleared soon after their arrival.

In between bites of his burger, James asked, "How long have you been taking Reggie's class?"

Anna swallowed. "Almost two years."

"That's it? Did you take self-defense classes before Reggie's class?"

Anna shook her head. "No. I had never even thrown a punch before. I still haven't thrown a punch outside of the gym."

"I've thrown a few punches, but it didn't go well for me. My record's 0-3." James shoved a fry with a little ketchup into his mouth.

Anna stared at his black eye. "Did they happen recently?"

James shook his head and swallowed. "No. I haven't been in a fight since I was a kid." This wasn't exactly true, but he didn't want to explain his fight with Matt. "Even then I did my best to avoid them. When I was in eighth grade, this kid was bullying me. Big kid named Carl. I mouthed off on the bus one afternoon, and he pummeled me at the bus stop. I was so petrified that I stopped riding the bus. I used to wake up forty-five minutes earlier than I used to so I could ride my bike to school. I may not be much of a fighter, but I'm still a pretty good bike rider."

"Did you tell your parents?"

"No. My mom would've been annoyed, and my stepfather probably would've beat me for getting my ass kicked."

Anna peered at James with a pained expression on her face. "I'm sorry, James."

James waved her off and dipped a fry in ketchup. "Don't be. It wasn't a big deal."

Anna scanned the diner, making sure the other patrons were out of earshot. "It is a big deal. I've been around a lot of DV victims. Almost all of them suffered abuse as children. Abusing a child doesn't only hurt that child in the moment but for the rest of their lives. They grow into adults who are more likely to be suicidal, addicted to drugs, and to be adult victims of DV."

"Well, thankfully I'm not any of those things."

Anna leaned forward. "Who gave you that black eye?"

James broke eye contact for a beat. "Ran into a doorframe. Walking and texting. Remember?"

"Can I be honest with you, James?"

He nodded.

"You sound exactly like a domestic violence victim. Full of excuses for the abuser. Who gave you that black eye?"

James dropped his fry and wiped his hands on his napkin. "I'm not a DV victim."

Anna arched her eyebrows.

"I'm *not*. I got into a fight with my brother-in-law."

"About what?"

"His sister. My wife." James stared at his plate. He spoke barely above a whisper. "She was murdered during a home invasion. He thinks I should've saved her, but I didn't."

"What do you think?" Anna asked, her voice kind.

"Not a minute goes by that I don't wish I had saved her, but I was asleep."

"I'm sorry, James."

James didn't respond.

"It's normal for survivors of violence to feel guilt, especially if someone close to them died in the event."

"I wish I could do it over."

Anna reached across the table and squeezed his hand. "I know the feeling, but you have to move forward. You have to forgive yourself. Whatever happened that night wasn't your fault."

James raised his gaze. "You know what happened?"

"Only what was in the *Lebanon Chronicle*. It was pretty big news. I read about it before we met."

James ran his hand over his face. "Does everyone in group know?"

"I imagine some people do, but we don't gossip about trauma. Everyone in group understands what it's like to be a survivor."

"But I didn't survive anything. I wasn't even hurt."

Anna shook her head again. "That's not true. You survived your wife's murder in your home. Just because you weren't physically harmed doesn't mean you weren't deeply wounded. Your trauma matters."

James forced a smile. "Thanks, Anna."

"You're welcome." Anna squeezed his hand one more time, then retracted hers.

"I keep thinking the guy knew Rachel. That was my wife's name."

"Do the police have any suspects?"

"I don't know. Last I heard, they told me they had some leads and that they weren't ruling anyone out. I actually found out that one of the detectives working her case used to be in love with Rachel in high school. Do you think that's a conflict of interest?"

"I don't know. It could be. I would ask him about it."

"I'm planning to."

"What about the guy who was shot?" Anna asked. "Are the police looking into his family and friends?"

THIRTY-FOUR
MRS. HENDERSON

HIS OLD GARMIN GPS navigated James to a middle-class neighborhood of ramblers and colonials built in the eighties. James found the address by running a background check on Quentin Henderson. It was a common last name, but there was only one *Quentin* Henderson nearby. James parked in front of a white colonial with black shutters and a two-car garage. It even had a white picket fence, with toys scattered about the front yard. Not what he was expecting from a criminal's house.

A girl, who appeared to be seven or eight, drove a pink Jeep around the lawn, while a slightly older boy whipped wiffle balls at the Jeep. They yelled back and forth at each other during the melee.

James exited his Honda and walked toward the house. It was warm, already in the low seventies. The kids wore shorts and t-shirts. They stopped their bickering to gawk as James followed the walkway to the front door. James pressed the doorbell.

A disheveled but attractive woman answered the door. "Can I help you?"

"Are you Leah Henderson?" James asked.

"Yes." She peered over James's shoulder, checking on her bickering children.

"I'm James Harris. Your husband—"

"I know who you are." She guarded the doorway. "What do you want?"

"I was wondering if I could ask you a few questions about your husband."

Leah craned her neck around James and yelled, "Bryce, be nice to your sister." She looked at James again. "I've already told the police everything I know."

"Would you mind telling me? Whoever killed your husband probably killed my wife."

Leah took a cleansing breath. Then she stepped onto the porch and shut the door behind her.

James stepped back, giving her room.

"What do you wanna know?"

"Did your husband have any friends or accomplices who might be capable of murder?"

Leah shook her head. "He never worked with hitmen. He was a safecracker, but he gave it all up for us years ago. He had a good job." She sniffed. "We were doing so well. His past … it was all in the past. This whole thing has been so … shocking."

"Why do you think he was involved?"

She wiped the corners of her eyes. "I don't know. He must've been forced somehow. Maybe someone was blackmailing him."

"What would they use for blackmail?"

She frowned. "My husband used to be a professional burglar. He had his skeletons."

James nodded. "Thank you for your time, Mrs. Henderson. May I leave my number with you in case you remember anything that might be important to the case?"

"Sure."

James grabbed his wallet from his back pocket and removed a business card. "If you give me your number, I'll do the same for you."

THIRTY-FIVE
ASKING QUESTIONS

THE NEXT MORNING James was on his hands and knees, pulling weeds from his garden and tossing them in a bucket bound for the compost pile. Despite his soreness from Reggie's self-defense class two days ago, he moved quickly, trying to beat the rain due by lunchtime. He glanced up at the darkening sky. *It may be sooner than lunchtime.*

As James worked, he thought about Rachel and the possibility that she was having an affair. *It must have something to do with her death. But why? If she was having an affair, I would be the most logical suspect.*

Gravel crunched under tires. James stood from his work. An unmarked police car parked in his driveway. James took off his gloves and walked toward the vehicle. Detective Decker exited the driver's side door. They met in the grass near the car.

"Good morning, Detective," James said.

Decker narrowed his eyes. "Heard you've been running around town, doing your own investigation."

"I wouldn't call it an investigation."

"What would you call it?"

"Asking questions."

Decker glared at James. "Do you want me to find your wife's killer?"

"If you wouldn't mind."

"Then don't run around town fucking up my investigation."

James crossed his arms over his chest. "Do you have any new leads?"

"It's an ongoing investigation. I'm not at liberty to discuss the case with potential suspects."

"I'm a suspect?"

"I haven't ruled you out."

James frowned. "What about her phone and her laptop? Did you find anything?"

Decker lifted his chin. "Like what?"

"Evidence of an affair."

"No."

James dropped his arms to his sides. "I'd like to have her phone and laptop back then."

"Not while the case is still open."

"I heard you were in love with Rachel in high school."

Decker's lips twitched. "I wouldn't say that. I had an unrequited crush, along with the rest of my male classmates—and probably some of the females too. But that's all in the distant past."

Sporadic raindrops fell from the black sky.

"Is it?" James asked.

"If you have something to say, say it," Decker replied.

James clenched his fists. "How am I supposed to trust that you're doing the right thing with Rachel's case if you're biased and emotionally involved?"

"I'm not biased, and I'm certainly not *emotional*, but if you want someone else to investigate her case, talk to Chief Tannehill. I've got nothing to hide. Until that time, stay away from my investigation."

The sporadic rain turned into a deluge, causing Decker to run for his car.

James called out to his back, "Do your job, Detective, and I won't do it for you."

THIRTY-SIX
TRUST

JAMES SLIPPED his jab and snapped his right cross. Satisfying *pops* came from the pads attached to Anna's hands.

"Nice, James. Keep it going," Reggie said as he walked by, checking his students.

James's shoulders were still sore from Thursday's class two days ago, but he punched a little harder and a little faster than last time. The timer buzzed and James dropped his hands, his upper body burning, his chest rising and falling with his elevated breathing.

"That was great. Nice work," Anna said, taking off the pads.

James smiled, despite the pain.

———

After class, James and Anna went to Mel's Diner again. Rain pelted the metal roof. They sat across from each other at a lonely booth, sipping their coffees.

"That detective, Frank Decker, came to my house this morning."

Anna set down her coffee cup. "Really? He's the one who was in love with Rachel when they were young, right?"

James nodded. "He came over to reprimand me for looking into the case. Told me to stop interfering."

"Were you interfering?"

"Remember when you mentioned talking to the family of the burglar who was shot in my house? I went to his house."

Her eyes widened. "I was thinking that the police would do that."

James scanned the diner, making sure nobody was within earshot. "I don't trust the police."

"Why not?"

James hesitated for a second, realizing he didn't want to admit that he didn't trust the police because they still viewed him as a suspect. "I don't think they're doing everything they can for Rachel. I feel compelled to do some digging myself."

Anna cradled her coffee cup in her hands. "That's understandable. Did you talk to the burglar's family?"

"I talked to his wife. Supposedly, her husband was a reformed criminal. He had a good job as a locksmith. Two young kids. Seems like he had a nice family. The wife thinks her husband was coerced into participating."

"Coerced by who?"

"She didn't say. I assume whoever organized the home invasion."

Anna leaned forward. "Maybe I've seen too many crime dramas, but do you think it's possible that it was an organized murder disguised as a burglary gone wrong?"

"Anything's possible." James rubbed the stubble on his chin, thinking about whether or not to share a secret. "I'd like to tell you something, but it's something that needs to stay between us."

"I hear a lot of privileged information at group. I'm not a gossip."

"I know." James hesitated for a moment. "I think Rachel might've been having an affair. To be clear, I don't know for sure if she was, but the night before it happened, she went out with her best friend. When she came home, I smelled cologne on her."

"Did you ask her about it?"

"She said her friend Ethan from high school gave her a hug right before she and her friend Liv left the bar. She said he had on a heavy amount of cologne."

"Sounds plausible."

"There's more. She had a bruise on her cheek."

Anna knitted her brow. "A bruise? From what?"

"I don't know. She gave me a bullshit excuse. I'm worried that she was having an affair with an abusive man. Maybe she realized she loved me and called it off. That could've set off the guy."

"I know you don't totally trust the police, but they should know about that."

"I'm not ready to trust them with that." In reality, James was worried that that information would make him a bigger suspect and, therefore, take valuable time and resources away from viable suspects. James wondered if the police already knew about the affair. After all, they had Rachel's cell phone. It would explain their continued interest in him as a suspect.

Anna nodded and sipped her coffee.

James's phone chimed in the front pocket of his sweatpants. He reached into his pocket, glanced at the name, and swiped left, sending Liv to voice mail.

"It's fine if you need to get that," Anna said.

James shoved his phone back into his pocket. "It's okay."

The waitress brought their food—chicken salads. As she set their food before them, James's phone buzzed in his pocket with a new text.

They ate in silence for several minutes.

"Rachel was a psychologist, right?" Anna asked.

James swallowed and set down his fork. "She was."

"What about her patients? You told me before that you thought the person knew her. Maybe one of her patients was fixated on her. We used to have an attorney in the group who was stalked by a former client."

"I went through her files—"

"Isn't that privileged information?" Anna asked.

James had a pained expression. "It is. I was … desperate. I thought the same thing as you, that maybe one of her patients was fixated on her. There is one guy who Rachel thought killed his first wife, but he has an alibi."

Anna narrowed her eyes. "Did you go see him?"

James nodded.

"That's really dangerous, James."

"I know."

She set down her fork. "I can't imagine how difficult this must be for you, but you need to be more careful. I'm not trying to scare you, but it's not out of the realm of possibility that you were also a target."

"I know. I'm not looking into her patients anymore."

"Good." She picked up her fork and took a bite of her salad.

James stared at her, touched by her concern for him. "Would you like to have dinner at my house?" He blurted out the invitation before he had time to second-guess himself.

She swallowed her food, nearly choking. She cleared her throat and said, "Are you sure that's a good idea? Your wife …" Anna trailed off.

James flushed, embarrassed. "I meant as friends. I don't really have anyone to talk to."

"When?"

"How about tomorrow night? I'm getting fresh salad greens and asparagus from my garden, and I have some grass-fed beef from my neighbor's cattle. I could grill."

THIRTY-SEVEN
THE HEART WANTS WHAT THE HEART WANTS

JAMES CLOSED the lid and set the grill to "smoke." The late-afternoon sun was high overhead. He faced Anna, who sat at the patio table, a glass of red wine before her. "It'll be about forty-five minutes. I hope you're not starving."

"I'm okay," Anna replied.

James sat across from her. Two citronella candles burned on the tabletop. A wooden privacy fenced surrounded them and the flagstone patio. "You were telling me about your sister."

Anna talked about her younger sister, who was happily married with a little boy. She also talked about her parents, who were still together and still in love. Her father worked for The Hershey Company in human resources, and her mother was a retired second-grade teacher.

"Have you ever been married?" James asked.

Anna's face darkened. "Once. It didn't work out."

"I'm sorry to hear that."

"I thought I'd have the perfect marriage, like my parents, but that wasn't ... in the cards." Anna forced a smile. "What about you? What's your family like?"

James glanced at the smoke coming from the grill and rising into the sky. "Not sure if this is polite dinner conversation."

"It's okay if you don't want to share."

"Like group?"

Anna smirked. "I guess."

"I come from a blended family. My father left when I was five. Never heard from him again. My mother remarried a guy who had two boys."

"How was that?"

James pressed his lips together in a flat line. "When I left for college, I never came back."

"*Never*? Not even for Christmas?"

"When I married Rachel, she talked me into reconciling, but that turned out to be a mistake."

"James," a woman called out, coming from outside the privacy fence.

James turned his head toward the voice. Liv opened the gate and entered the backyard, holding a covered dish, wearing heels and a tight skirt. She tottered on the stepping stones toward the patio, the irregular stones providing a precarious path for someone with her footwear. Liv had been so focused on James that she hadn't seen Anna, and then she did.

Liv gaped at Anna, her momentum still moving her forward on the stepping stones, but she missed the stone with her left foot, her heel sinking into the grass, causing her to wobble. The covered dish slipped from her grasp. The thick glass shattered on a stone, a split second before Liv fell face forward. Her hands stopped her face from smashing into a stone, but her body fell on her food.

"Oh my God," Anna said, standing.

James rushed to help Liv. "Are you okay?"

Liv winced. "I think so."

James helped her up. Red sauce from the eggplant parmesan stained her khaki skirt. One of her knees was red with a brush burn but not nearly as red as her face.

Liv gaped at Anna. She spoke in a monotone. "I tried to call. I didn't know you had company."

"You're bleeding," James said. "Let's get you cleaned up."

"I'm so sorry." Liv reached down and removed her heels. "I have to go."

"Let's go inside—"

Liv pivoted and ran from the backyard in her bare feet.

"Liv," James called out. "You don't have to go."

"Who was that?" Anna asked.

"Rachel's best friend. I was supposed to call her. She wanted to talk to me about something."

The day before, while James and Anna ate at the diner, Liv had left James a voice message and had sent a text. Her voice message had said, "Hi, James. It's Liv. Call me when you get this. It's important. I'd like to come by. I don't wanna say anything over the phone." Her text had been a repeat of the voice message. James had planned to return her call, but he had been preoccupied with Anna, and he wasn't sure if he wanted to hear any more about Rachel's high school skeletons.

———

Several hours later, two bottles of wine sat empty on the patio table. The citronella candles and the moon provided the only light. Their plates were empty. Only a little fat and gristle remained from their steaks.

Anna downed the last of her wine. Her words were slightly slurred. "I think Liv's in love with you."

"I hope not," James replied, his senses dulled from the wine. "She's a good friend. I'd hate to lose that."

"The heart wants what the heart wants."

"Think so, *huh*?"

Anna grinned, shadows dancing on her face. "I know so."

"What does your heart want?"

She giggled. "Wouldn't you like to know."

James deadpanned, "I wouldn't ask if I didn't want to know. Seriously, what do you want for your life?"

"I don't know." Her smile evaporated. "I used to think I knew, but I don't know anymore."

"What did you want when you thought you knew?"

"I guess what every woman wants, a handsome husband, two point five kids, and a white picket fence. What about you?"

"I thought I had everything I ever wanted." James stared at one of the candles.

They were silent for a long moment.

Anna glanced at her phone. "Oh my God, it's past midnight. I should go before I turn into a pumpkin."

"You can't drive," James said. "I don't think I should drive either."

"I guess I could get an Uber. I don't have the app though. Do you?"

"No, but I have two guest bedrooms and a brand-new toothbrush still in the package."

THIRTY-EIGHT
FIGHT, FLIGHT, OR FREEZE

JAMES WAS ON HIS KNEES, showing his shaking palms. The man in the mask aimed his handgun at James's head.

"Please don't shoot," James said. "I'll do anything."

Rachel knelt next to James, also begging. "Please don't hurt me. Whatever this is, we can figure it out. Please."

The man in the mask aimed his handgun at Rachel, then James, then Rachel, then back to James. He said in a deep voice, "Choose."

"I can't," James said.

"Choose or you both die."

James closed his eyes and said, "Her." He flinched at the gunshot, his ears ringing. When James opened his eyes, Rachel lay on her side, motionless, blood spilling from the hole in her head.

The man removed his mask. It was Nathan Mills, Rachel's former client, the black widower. He aimed his handgun at James again and said, "Fucking coward." Then he pulled the trigger.

James thrashed in his bed, shouting, "No! Don't shoot! Stop!" He was drenched in sweat. The guest bedroom came into focus. The ceiling fan rotated overhead. Moonlight slipped between the blinds in slivers. His breathing regulated.

Footsteps came from the hallway. A knock came at the door, causing James to startle.

"James?" Anna called out.

"I'm fine," James replied, his voice shaky.

"May I come in?"

"I'm fine."

"I'm coming in." She waited for a second, then pushed inside the bedroom. Anna approached his bedside, wearing the sweats James had let her borrow. "Are you okay? You were shouting."

James sat up in bed and flipped on the bedside table lamp. "I'm okay."

"You don't look okay. Let me get you a towel." She went into the attached bathroom and returned with a towel. She handed James the towel and sat on the edge of the bed.

James dried his sweat.

"Is this a regular occurrence?"

James set the towel in his lap. "Every night since it happened."

"I'm sorry."

"Don't be. I'm the one who should be sorry." James squeezed the towel. "I lied to the police. I lied to everyone. I was awake when she was killed, and I did nothing." James stared at the towel in his lap. "I'm a coward."

Anna reached out and took his hand. "You were in an incredibly traumatic situation, and you froze. It's far more common than you might think. It doesn't make you a coward. It makes you human."

"I wish I could go back …"

"Don't do that. It wasn't your fault."

"I can't shake the guilt."

"I know exactly how you feel. I froze too, just like you did."

James lifted his gaze to Anna. "You did?"

Anna nodded. "It was three years ago. I was leaving work. It was March, so tax time was in full gear, and I was stressed and distracted and four months' pregnant. It was late. I was the last one to leave the office. The parking garage was mostly empty. I had my laptop over my shoulder because I had planned to work from home over the weekend." Anna took a deep breath. "I remember digging in my purse, annoyed that I couldn't find my keys. I finally found my keys after a minute. I unlocked my doors, and that's when the man grabbed me from behind and put a knife to my neck."

James squeezed Anna's hand, his eyes like saucers.

"I froze. I didn't even make a sound. I let that piece of shit rape me in the back of my car, and I did *nothing*. It wasn't the rape that ruined my life. It was what happened afterward. I had PTSD. I was depressed. My husband was angry about the whole thing. Wanted to kill the guy. He blamed me for working too late, for being too stupid, for not fighting back." Anna sniffled and exhaled. "I went from a confident woman, who seemingly had it all, to a broken woman with nothing. I had nightmares, like you. Mostly, I blamed myself for freezing, for letting that man do what he wanted to me without any resistance. The police never found him. I was so traumatized that I couldn't even give them a decent description."

"I'm so sorry, Anna."

Anna lifted one shoulder. "Ironically, the first thing I learned in Reggie's class is to have your keys in hand, ready to go." She sighed, her eyes glassy. "A few weeks after the rape, I had a miscarriage. My husband …" Anna wiped the corners of her eyes.

James swallowed the lump in his throat. "What happened to your husband?"

"We separated a few months later. Divorced a few months after that. He's remarried now. Seems happy, if you believe everything you see on Facebook."

"That's awful. I don't know what to say."

Anna gazed at James, unblinking. "There's nothing to say. I'm telling you this because I want you to know that I understand what it's like to freeze and lose everything you've ever cared about. I understand how that can happen. I used to blame myself, just like you, but it's not right. My rapist is to blame for my trauma. Those men who broke into your house are to blame for yours. That's it. You have *nothing* to feel guilty about."

THIRTY-NINE
UNREQUITED

A SHADOW PASSED over James's face. His eyelids fluttered and opened. Anna's face, clean and beautiful without makeup, looked down on him. She sat on the edge of his bed, dressed in her sundress from the night before.

She said, "Thank you for letting me stay last night."

James sat upright in bed. He glanced at the alarm clock. It was 8:22 a.m. "Are you leaving?"

"I should get out of your hair."

"No. Please stay in my hair."

She smiled. "I should go."

"At least let me make you breakfast."

Anna pursed her lips.

"C'mon. It's Saturday," James said.

———

James dipped the bread in egg. Then he set the bread on the skillet with three others.

"Smells wonderful," Anna said, sitting at the center island on a barstool.

James looked over his shoulder and grinned. "Tastes even

better. I have real maple syrup too. I have a friend who has family from Ohio with a maple syrup farm."

James's cell phone buzzed with a text. Then another text.

"I think someone's texting you," Anna said.

James flipped the French toast. "I'm sure it can wait."

James served coffee, ice water, and a fruit salad with the French toast. He sat across from Anna at the dining room table. They enjoyed their breakfast, talking about their favorite movies. James's favorites were *The Shawshank Redemption*, *Heartbreak Kid*, and *It's a Wonderful Life*. Anna's favorites were *Titanic*, *Forest Gump*, *Good Will Hunting*, and *The Goonies*.

James laughed. "*The Goonies*? Are you ten?"

Anna mock-frowned. "Don't be a movie snob. *The Goonies* was a great movie. Kids' movies are usually better than movies for adults. *Shrek* is definitely in my top ten."

James's cell phone buzzed with another text. He glanced at the notification on his screen. It was from a colleague at Lebanon Valley College.

"What is it?" Anna asked.

"It's from someone I work with," James replied. "He rarely ever texts me. Do you mind if I check his message?"

"Go ahead."

James tapped to his messages. He had three new texts from three different people who worked with him at Lebanon Valley College. James read the latest one.

Timothy Naylor: I hate to be the bearer of bad news, but I was wondering if you heard about Liv? She was found dead in her bathtub this morning. An apparent suicide.

James frantically checked the other messages, hoping Timothy was wrong, that he was mistaken, but they confirmed it.

"What's wrong?" Anna asked.

James looked up from his phone, his eyes glassy. "Liv's dead."

FORTY
GOODBYE, LIV

FIVE DAYS LATER, on Cinco de Mayo, James waited in line to see Liv's dead body. James shuffled with the line until he reached Liv's parents, who waited just before the casket.

James shook hands with Liv's parents, his stomach churning underneath his calm exterior. "I'm James Harris. I worked with your daughter. She was a great friend."

"Thank you so much for coming," her father said.

"Of course. My condolences."

The mother narrowed her eyes at James. "You're Rachel's husband."

James bowed his head. "I was."

The mother blanched. "I'm sorry."

"It's okay. Who knows what to say in these situations?"

"Liv liked you. Told me you brought her a cake on her birthday."

James said, "I liked her too. She was a good friend."

The mother hugged James. "Thank you for coming."

"You're welcome."

James moved beyond the parents, letting the next person in line express their condolences. The shiny mahogany casket was open. Liv wore a black dress and gold jewelry. Her face was puffy and caked with makeup. Her eyes were closed. James thought, *I'm so sorry, Liv*. His throat constricted and his eyes watered. James pivoted and left the room, his head down to conceal his emotions.

He went to the bathroom and washed his face. He left the bathroom and the funeral home. On his way to the parking lot, he spotted Damon in the funeral garden. The Japanese garden was a great spot to grieve, with a koi pond and a small recirculating waterfall. Japanese maples provided dappled shade.

James walked on the paver pathway to Damon, who sat on the bench, watching the koi. "Hey, Damon."

Damon glanced at James and nodded.

"I'm sorry about your cousin."

Damon nodded again, his eyes on the koi.

James pivoted to leave, but Damon said, "She was one of the few people who gave a shit about me."

James turned back to Damon. "She was a good friend."

"She was more than that."

"You're right." James hesitated for a second. "A few weeks ago, she told me about how you jumped into the quarry in high school. She said you were braver than the football stars."

Damon grinned at James. "That was a long time ago."

"She told me Frank Decker was there too."

Damon's smile evaporated. "Yeah. He was there."

"You didn't like him?"

"Still don't."

James stepped closer to Damon. "Why not?"

"The problem with going to school in a small town is you're in the same classes with the same people year after year. If someone's an asshole, you can't get away from them."

"What the fuck are you doing here?" Matt shouted as he marched into the Japanese garden.

James faced the oncoming hurricane. Without thought, he assumed the fighting position he had learned in Reggie's class. As soon as Matt reached striking distance, James threw a hard jab followed by a right cross. One, two. *Pop, pop*. The jab caught the fleshy cartilage of Matt's nose and the cross landed on his chin, sending him down for the count.

Damon left the scene, hurrying away from the crime.

Matt writhed on the ground, holding his bloody nose. "What the fuck did you do that for?"

James stared at his hands as if they weren't his. Then James hurried away from the scene, realizing Matt wasn't expecting another fistfight and James may have committed assault. On the way to his car, James saw Damon again. As he fast-walked past, Damon gave him a subtle thumbs-up.

James climbed into his car and drove away, his tires chirping and his heart still pounding. He stopped at a red light, and his cell phone chimed.

He reached into his inside jacket pocket, retrieved his cell phone, and swiped right. "Hello?"

"Is this James Harris?" The male voice sounded familiar.

"Yes."

"This is Philip Kennedy. Your coin is gone." Phillip Kennedy was Rachel's former patient, the one with the shady cryptocurrency fund.

"What do you mean, it's gone?"

The light turned green, and James drove through the intersection.

"All I can say is, it's been sold and resold and resold. It's gone," Philip said.

"Did you find out anything about the original seller?" James asked.

"The dealer paid with Bitcoin, so no credit card trail. No address either. The seller did give a name, but I'm sure it's fake."

"What was the name?"

"Raymond."

FORTY-ONE
RAYMOND

ON SATURDAY, James held the door open for Anna as they left the YMCA. They strolled to the parking lot, the sun warming their skin.

"Did you want to go to the diner?" James asked.

"Maybe for just a cup of coffee," Anna replied. "It's my nephew's birthday. There's a party at my sister's house. Apparently, there's a bouncy house."

"Sounds fun."

Anna smirked. "Not for the adults."

James pointed to his Honda Accord. "I can drive. I'll bring you back, unless you want to leave directly from the diner."

"I'm happy to ride with you. I have to come back this way anyway, but it's out of *your* way."

"I don't mind." He almost told Anna that he would gladly backtrack for a few extra minutes with her, but he didn't know how she'd take an obvious pass, and he wasn't ready to admit his attraction for another woman only one month after Rachel's death.

As they drove toward the diner, James said, "Did I ever tell you that whoever killed Rachel also stole my coin collection?"

Anna turned in the passenger seat toward James. "No. I knew there was a burglary, but I didn't know what they took."

James glanced from the road to Anna, then back again. "I had one coin that was worth quite a lot. One of Rachel's patients used to be in the rare coin business. He was one of the patients who I looked into. I don't think he had anything to do with it, but he's a pretty shady guy, so I figured he might know a local dealer who would buy stolen coins." James stopped the car at a four-way stop, letting two cars go before him. "I asked him to let me know if he hears about someone trying to sell the coin."

"Did he hear something?" Anna asked.

James drove through intersection. "All he got was a name."

"A *name*?" Anna sounded excited.

James glanced at Anna and shook his head. "It doesn't mean anything. It was *Raymond*, but it was probably a fake name. I don't know any Raymonds. I don't think Rachel did either. I even went back to her patient files. She doesn't have a single patient named Ray or Raymond."

"What about your coin?"

James shook his head again. "It's gone. Sold and resold several times already. Off the books and paid for with Bitcoin."

"What's next?"

"I don't know. I'm out of leads. I'm hoping the police find something."

FORTY-TWO
TWO MONTHS LATER ...

SUNRAYS FILTERED through the tree canopy. Cicadas buzzed overhead. A squirrel zipped up a large oak tree. James and Anna hiked uphill on the rocky trail.

"I spoke with Detective Banks," James said.

Anna stepped onto a large flat rock and pivoted to James. "When?"

James joined her on the rock. "Yesterday. He admitted that the case is dead. It's not closed, but they aren't actively following any leads either."

"I'm sorry."

James shrugged. "Me too."

Anna hugged him and said, "It's okay to let go."

When they separated, James said, "It's hard to let go. Especially after I ..."

"You have to stop punishing yourself."

He exhaled. "Easier said than done."

She frowned, but it wasn't anger in her eyes. It was sadness.

James motioned toward the trail. "How much farther?"

"We're almost there."

They hiked in silence. James thought about the past two

months with Anna. She had been his confidant and friend. His best friend. His only friend. He was attracted to her, but the better friends they became, the more he felt he had to lose by making a move, not to mention James's love for Rachel. What was the appropriate amount of time to wait before dating again? So James had settled into the friend zone.

He saw Anna at group and Reggie's self-defense class. James never missed either, although he still hadn't shared in group. They went to the diner afterward for coffee and sometimes dinner. They hiked together. They ate at each other's houses, but they didn't sleep over, not since the first and last time two months ago. Not since Liv had killed herself.

Anna turned left, off the trail. She grinned and said, "This is it." She turned sideways and squeezed through two boulders the size of SUVs. James peered into the narrow space, which was about two feet wide, but appeared smaller.

"Come on," Anna said from the other side.

James turned sideways and shuffled between the boulders, feeling the cold stone wall as he went. He emerged from the dark hallway to the bright sun. He stood on a massive stone ledge, scanning the blue skies above and the green valley below.

"Isn't it beautiful?" Anna asked.

James turned his attention to Anna. The sun formed a halo behind her head. Her brown eyes held flecks of gold. "Thank you."

"For what?"

"For being my friend. I don't know what I would've done without you."

"It goes both ways."

James took a deep breath of mountain air. "I'll never forget, but you're right. I have to let go. I can't live in this self-imposed purgatory. It's time for me to move forward."

She smiled. "The end can also be a new beginning."

"I hope so." James edged closer to her, expecting her to step back, but she didn't move. He expected her to flinch when he put his hands on her hips, but she didn't. He expected her to recoil as he leaned in for the kiss, but she reciprocated. She reciprocated as if she had been waiting two months for him to finally make a move.

FORTY-THREE
NORMAL?

THEY HELD hands as they hiked back to the trailhead. James wondered if the kiss meant they were a couple. It had been so long since he had dated that it felt very foreign to him. Was he supposed to express his desire for exclusivity? Although, he was certain she wasn't seeing anyone else and hadn't for a long time. There had been a guy after her husband, but it had quickly fizzled. Anna hadn't been descriptive, only saying that it hadn't worked out.

They loitered in the gravel parking lot, near their cars.

James still held her hand, not wanting to let her go. "What are you doing for the rest of the day?"

She blushed. "Hopefully, going home with you."

They drove separately to James's house.

James ushered Anna inside, butterflies in his stomach and his heart pounding. Anna kissed James as soon as he shut the front door. Their teeth clicked together because of their urgency. She smelled like the sun, with a faint smell of sweet sweat. They turned around, and James pressed his body against her, mashing her against the front door. He pinned her arms to the door and kissed her neck. Anna stiffened and James relented.

"Are you okay?" James asked.

"I'm fine." Anna slipped her hand down the front of James's sweatpants. He groaned in response to her squeezing his penis.

"I want you," he breathed into her ear.

He led her to the couch, unconcerned about the open curtains, as visitors were infrequent, and the neighbors were distant.

Standing in front of the couch, they alternated between kissing, touching, and disrobing. Anna lifted her arms so James could remove her t-shirt, exposing her white sports bra. James kicked off his sneakers and removed his t-shirt. Anna slipped off her socks and sneakers. James slipped his hand under her spandex pants and underwear, touching her slick clitoris. Anna gasped and shuddered. His erection pressed against her thigh, hard enough to toe the line between pleasure and pain.

"Do we need a condom?" James asked breathlessly.

She nodded.

"I'll be right back." James bolted upstairs, grabbed a condom from the medicine cabinet, and returned to the living room.

They picked up where they left off, kissing and disrobing. James removed his pants and underwear like they were on fire. Anna's hands trembled, as she slid her spandex pants and underwear down her toned legs. Now naked before him, she covered her small breasts with one arm, the other covering her crotch.

"What's wrong?" James asked.

"Nothing," Anna replied. She lay on the couch and spread her legs. Her face was taut; her eyes were glassy.

James knelt before her and rolled the condom down his penis. He scooched forward and placed the head of his penis inside her. Then he lay atop her and pushed inside her.

Her body went rigid. She squeezed her eyes shut.

"What's wrong?" James asked, no longer moving inside her.

Anna took shallow quick breaths. She pressed against James's chest. Her words were frantic. "I can't breathe. I can't breathe." She shouted, "Get off me! Get off me!"

James recoiled and pulled out, quickly standing, then kneeling next to her.

She sat up and pulled her knees to her chest. Tears streamed down her face.

"What's wrong?"

"I'm sorry."

"It's okay. There's nothing to be sorry about." James grabbed the decorative blanket from the couch and wrapped it around Anna. Then he slipped on his sweatpants, covering himself.

Anna rocked under the covers, sobbing.

James sat next to her and held her, letting her cry onto his shoulder.

When she finished, she wriggled from his embrace and said, "I should go."

"Please don't."

She wiped the corners of her eyes with her index finger. "I don't know if I'll ever be normal."

"What does *normal* even mean?"

"Don't you want someone who can have sex without freaking out?"

"I want you."

FORTY-FOUR
ONE MONTH LATER ...

SUNLIGHT FILTERED through the sheer curtains in James's guest bedroom. On a lazy Sunday morning, James and Anna lay in bed, their chests rising and falling. A breeze came from the ceiling fan. An aluminum bat leaned against the bedpost. Their phones cuddled on the bedside table, plugged in to their chargers. James and Rachel used to leave their cell phones in the kitchen to prevent overuse before bed, which could interrupt sleep patterns, but now James viewed his cell phone as a potential safety item, necessary to keep nearby.

Anna rolled on to James, her head nuzzled in his neck. He wrapped his arm around her and squeezed her tight to his body.

James kissed the crown of her head. "Are you okay?"

"Yes," she replied.

"You sure? I wasn't sure whether or not to …"

"I wanted you to keep going."

"That's what you said, but you felt"—James winced as he said—"tense."

She tilted her head to him. "I was a little tense, but I still wanted you. I haven't felt that with anyone since before …"

James kissed her on the lips. "I love you."

She smiled. "I love you too."

James held her, their breathing synchronized, her soft skin pressed against his, breathing in her pheromones and her fruity shampoo.

"I wish I could stay like this forever," Anna said.

"I don't have anywhere to be for three weeks," James replied. Fall term started on August 29.

"I wish I didn't have to go to work tomorrow."

"You don't. Take a day off."

"I can't. We're short-staffed, and you know I'm up for partner."

"Well, we have today. We'll do anything you want."

"Let's do this again and again, but first let's have French toast and bacon and peaches with whipped cream."

James and Anna had picked fresh flame-red peaches the day before.

He gave her one last kiss, then slipped out of bed. "How about breakfast in bed?"

―――

James whisked the eggs as Anna skipped into the kitchen.

"You were supposed to wait upstairs," James said.

Anna pouted. "I missed you." She rose to her tippy toes and pecked him on the cheek. Then she gave him a quick hug from behind and said, "I'll cut the peaches."

Anna grabbed a cutting board and sliced clingstone peaches while James worked on the French toast. While cooking, they took every opportunity to kiss and caress each other, as couples did during the honeymoon phase of a relationship.

Anna grabbed the whipped cream from the fridge and set it on the center island, next to two bowls of cut peaches. She ate a peach slice, then kissed him on the lips, swirling her tongue around his. She tasted like the sweet fruit. When they separated, she said, "We're one of those annoying couples, aren't we?"

"What are you talking about?" James asked.

"You know. Those couples who are all over each other."

He reached out and pulled her into an embrace. "Only if we do this in public."

She peered up at him. "Last night we were holding hands across the dinner table."

They had gone out to The Harvest Moon last night, a farm-to-table local restaurant.

"Maybe we *are* one of those couples," James said, giving Anna one last squeeze before letting her go.

She giggled. "I think I'm making *myself* ill."

James turned on a stovetop burner. "Speak for yourself. I like being one of those couples."

"Now we need one of those celebrity couple names, like Bennifer."

James dipped a slice of bread into the egg. "What's a Bennifer?" James tossed the egg-saturated bread into the pan.

"Bennifer was Ben Affleck and Jennifer Lopez. Brangelina was another one. That was Brad Pitt and Angelina Jolie. We could be Janna. Or Ames. I think I prefer Janna." She grinned and shoved a peach into her mouth.

James stepped back from the stove, slack-jawed.

"What's wrong?" Anna asked.

"Holy shit."

"What is it?"

"Remember the name of the person who sold my coin?"

"It was Raymond, right?"

James nodded. "What if it wasn't Raymon*d* with a *D* at the end, but it was *Raymon* without the *D*? What if it was Rachel and Damon put together?"

Anna's eyes widened in recognition. "Oh my God."

FORTY-FIVE
BENNIFER AND BRANGELINA

JAMES TAPPED Detective Banks's contact, automatically dialing his cell phone. James paced in the kitchen while Anna looked on.

"Detective Banks here," he said.

"This is James Harris. I'm sorry to bother you on a Sunday, but I have some important information about Rachel's case."

Banks exhaled. "I'm listening."

"I heard from a reliable source that my coin was sold by someone named *Raymon*."

"Did you say Raymond?"

"No. *Raymon*, without the *D* at the end."

"Is there someone connected to your wife named *Raymon*?"

"No, but if you put the name together like one of those celebrity couples, like Bennifer was Ben Affleck and Jennifer Lopez, well, *Raymon* could be Rachel and Damon, as in Damon Williams, who's a foreman at Taylor Construction, who was in love with Rachel since they were kids."

There was no response for several seconds.

"Detective Banks?"

The detective sounded weary. "Yeah. I'm here."

"What do you think?" James asked.

Banks cleared his throat. "Who is this source? Is he someone I can interview?"

"He won't talk, but I'm pretty sure he's telling the truth."

"Do you have any evidence other than his word?"

"Not really."

"Not really, or no?"

James plopped on the barstool at the center island next to Anna, his shoulders slumped. "No."

Anna rubbed his back, listening to the conversation.

Banks said, "Let me get this straight. You have a first name of someone who sold your coin, but you don't know if the name is fake or if the person who told you the name is telling the truth."

James swallowed. "*Uh*, … I suppose so."

"And even if the name is correct, it doesn't match anyone who your wife knew, but it might match someone if we chop the name up into parts, like a celebrity couple name?"

"I know it sounds crazy, but you have to understand. Damon was in love with Rachel. People who are in love do stuff like this."

"This isn't a lead, James. I can't do anything with this information."

"You could question Damon."

"We've already questioned him. I don't think he had anything to do with it."

"Did he have an alibi?"

"It's not a crime to live alone."

"Will you please talk to him again?"

"I'll look into it," Banks replied.

"When?" James asked.

"I don't know. I have a lot of cases at the moment, but I'll get to it within the next week or two."

James gritted his teeth. "That's not good enough."

"It'll have to be." Detective Banks disconnected the call.

James slapped his phone on the center island. "He doesn't give a shit."

"Maybe it is a stretch," Anna said. "He's right. There's no evidence that your information's true."

James shook his head. "I don't know how to explain it, but I think Philip Kennedy is telling the truth."

"But even then, we don't know that Damon made up the name. We're guessing based on some tabloid fad."

"I need to talk to Damon."

"Please don't." Anna stood from the barstool and rotated James's stool to face her. "It could be dangerous."

"I'll be fine."

"You don't know that. If he's innocent, you'll be fine. If he's not, you'll be in serious danger. At least give Detective Banks a couple of weeks to interview him."

James dropped his gaze. "Okay."

Anna put her hand under his chin and raised his gaze to meet hers. "Promise me you won't go over there."

"*Okay.*"

FORTY-SIX
THE QUARRY

ON MONDAY AFTERNOON, while Anna went to work, James drove on a gravel road through the woods. A rusty sign read Lebanon Marble Quarry. Wintercreeper snaked up the posts and partially covered the sign.

James slowed his car to a crawl as he neared a mailbox and a singlewide trailer. The name on the mailbox read Damon Williams. A brand-new Ford F-150 with thirty-day tags was parked in the driveway. *Did he pay for that with my gold double eagle?* James had figured Damon would likely be at work on the second Monday in August. He had hoped to snoop around his house without being disturbed.

Maybe he uses a company truck to commute to work.

James reversed his car and parked along the woods, about fifty-meters away from the metal trailer. He cut through the woods, exiting through blackberry brambles that caught his jeans, to enter Damon's backyard. Motors and lawn and construction equipment were scattered throughout the yard in various stages of repair.

James crept to the rear window of the trailer and peered inside. Wood paneling and dirty beige carpet lined the living room. A flat-screen television sat before a gaming chair and a gaming console. The screen was paused on a first-person shooter game. James dipped under the window, realizing Damon was likely home.

"What are you doing?" Damon asked, his voice coming from the backyard.

James flinched and turned to Damon, standing upright. "Sorry. I didn't think anyone was home."

Damon stepped closer, within twenty feet. "Why are you looking in my window?"

"I was looking for you."

"For what?"

"I wanted to ask you a few questions."

"Go home." Damon turned to leave.

"Are you *Raymon*?" James asked.

Damon turned back to James, his brow furrowed. "What?"

"When you sold my gold double eagle to buy your new truck, you used the name *Raymon*. It's a hybrid of Rachel and Damon, isn't it?"

Damon's jaw tensed for a split second, then he said, "I don't know what you're talking about."

"I know what you did." James stalked closer, his fists clenched, unafraid of Damon's small stature.

Damon reached behind his back, grabbed his handgun, and aimed it at James.

James sucked in a sharp breath, stopped in his tracks, and showed his palms. "Relax. No need to do that."

Damon motioned with his gun. "Let's go."

"Where are we going?"

Damon motioned toward the woods. "Let's go."

James's hands trembled. "You don't have to do this."

Damon racked the slide on his handgun, chambering a round. Then he aimed the gun at James again. "If you don't move, I'll shoot you right here."

James walked toward the woods, roughly where Damon had pointed. Damon followed. As James neared the woods, he noticed a trail.

"Right there," Damon said. "Take the trail."

James walked slowly, hoping to stay alive long enough to find a way out of the situation. "Why are you doing this?"

Damon didn't answer.

James hiked on the narrow trail through the woods, Damon close behind. The afternoon sun was high overhead; beams of light cut through the forest canopy.

"It's not my fault Rachel didn't love you," James said.

"She didn't love you either," Damon replied.

James glanced over his shoulder to Damon. "How do you know that?"

Damon hesitated for a second, then said, "She wanted me to kill you."

James stopped, his face taut. He turned to Damon. "What are you talking about?"

"Keep walking." Damon gestured with his handgun.

"What are you talking about?"

"Keep walking and I'll tell you."

James pivoted and continued on the trail at a snail's pace.

Damon said, "She convinced me to do it. Said you were abusing her and needed my help. Said she loved me and that we could be together, if I got rid of you."

"That's bullshit. She thought you were a loser—"

"You're right. She did think I was a loser, but she never thought I'd figure her out."

"What did you figure out?"

"That she's a manipulative bitch. That she was just using me."

James scanned the forest without turning his head, checking for anything that might help him escape. An errant hiker. A crevice he could jump into. Anything.

"I have a question." Damon didn't wait for James to respond. "What kind of husband lets his wife die? You must've heard her crying for help, yet you did nothing."

James gritted his teeth.

Damon continued. "She thought I was a loser, yet she married you, a pathetic coward. No wonder she wanted you dead."

The trail opened to a rocky cliff, with a steep drop to the marble quarry and the dark blue water below.

"Stop right there," Damon said.

James stopped about fifteen feet from the edge. A rock the size of a soccer ball sat on the edge with a U-bolt drilled into it, and a chain attached to the U-bolt. At the end of the chain was a metal cuff with an open lock. James's eyes widened in recognition. He thought about running and jumping off the cliff. But Damon moved in front of James, standing between him and the edge, still with his handgun trained on James.

"I thought you might show up here months ago. Or that fuck-tard Decker." Damon bent down and grabbed the end of the chain with the cuff. He stepped closer to James, holding the gun in one hand, the chain in the other. The chain was taut, barely reaching James. "Sit down. On your ass."

James stared at the cuff with the little padlock, calculating the events to come. It wasn't even a thought, but a visceral feeling that, if that cuff made it around his ankle, he would drown. The gun was vaguely aimed in James's direction with one hand.

With the quickness of a viper, James slapped the gun and bolted for the edge. Damon fired three times. The first shot was errant after James had slapped the gun. The second bit his left shoulder, just before he leapt from the cliff. The third snapped past his left ear.

His arms windmilled, as if trying to fly. James was weightless, the water below fast approaching. He crashed through the glassy blue surface, water spraying into his nose, his momentum taking him into the depths. Below him was darkness. Above, sunlight filtered into the water. He tried to swim to the surface, but his first pull with his arms sent a shooting pain throughout his left shoulder. He kicked his legs and used his right arm, surfacing with a ragged choking breath. He coughed, spat, and sucked in air.

A gunshot cracked from above, the bullet zipping past him

into the water. James looked up. Damon aimed his handgun from the ledge one hundred feet above. Another gunshot snapped past James, close enough to feel the energy. James kicked to the marble wall, pulling with his right arm, placing himself underneath the ledge, making it impossible for Damon to shoot him from above.

The marble wall was nearly sheer, cut by machines long ago. Impossible to climb, even if James hadn't been shot. James braced himself against the wall with his good arm, still kicking to keep his head above water. Weighed down by boots and clothes, treading water was tiresome.

James scanned the old quarry. It was surrounded by marble walls, like a fortress. Across the pool from James was a single entry and exit point—a steep but manageable slope that had been used by the miners. James calculated his options. If he stayed where he was, he would tire from blood loss and eventually drown. Damon would likely go to the entry to wait for James and finish the job, unless James made it there first.

He sidestroked away from the wall, scissoring his legs and pulling with his right arm. His left shoulder burned with each stroke, despite not using his left arm. James glanced back at the cliff edge, expecting Damon to take another shot at him, but he was gone.

With James halfway across the quarry pool, Damon appeared at the entry, his gun held out front. Damon hurried to the water's edge. James and Damon locked eyes. Damon aimed his gun and James submerged. The *pop* of the gunshot was muffled by the water. James kicked and swam underwater back toward the quarry wall, as far from Damon as possible.

When James surfaced, Damon fired again, the bullet snapping over his head. James went under again, kicking and pulling with one arm, adrenaline propelling him through the water. He swam underwater until he had nearly passed out from a lack of oxygen. James surfaced and inhaled deeply. Not waiting for another gunshot, James submerged again and swam underwater until he reached the quarry wall.

About two hundred meters of water separated James from Damon, who now sat on a large rock on the shore, content to wait for James to perish from blood loss, exhaustion, or some combination of the two.

James tried to cling to the marble wall but found no toeholds or handholds in the sheer wall. So, he tread water, moving his legs like a cyclist and waving one hand through the water. He played with his level of exertion, expending as little effort as possible to keep his nose above water, all the while watching Damon at the shore, ready to submerge if need be. He thought about floating on his back, but he couldn't do that *and* watch Damon.

He remembered his cell phone, reaching down and feeling his front pocket. It was still there, held in place by the tight pocket. He grunted, his left shoulder barking in pain as he twisted, using his right hand to grab the phone from the left front pocket of his jeans. The screen was black. He tried to wake the phone, but it was dead, the electronics waterlogged.

―――

It was hard to tell how long it had been. It felt like many hours, but James guessed he had been in the water for one hour. His legs were exhausted and cramping. The left side of his upper body was stiff, his shoulder grinding in pain with even subtle movements. His right arm and shoulder burned from fatigue. His vision was fuzzy. He was drowsy. He thought about swimming for shore. Letting Damon shoot him. It would be a better death than drowning, but he doubted he had the energy to make it.

James dipped under, too exhausted to kick anymore. He held his breath, but not for long. When he sucked in the water, adrenaline coursed through his body, causing him to kick and buck to the surface, choking and coughing and sucking in air. He did this several times, slipping under, nearly drowning, only for his body to revolt, for adrenaline to push him to the surface again.

Until he couldn't do it anymore. Until he finally reached his physical limit. The blackness came from the edges of his vision until he was gone. He slipped under again. A heavy splash jostled him, waking him again. He kicked once. Twice. Just enough to break the surface, but he didn't break the surface. Something held him under. He flailed, the last gasps of a dying man.

Then he was gone.

FORTY-SEVEN
AFTER THE PLUNGE

THE ROOM WAS BLURRY. James's mind was hazy, like he was in a dream or a nightmare. *Where am I?*

"He's waking up," someone said.

Something was in his throat. He thrashed and choked. He was drowning. His left shoulder burned with pain when he moved. Strong hands held him steady as the tube was removed from his sore throat.

Dark forms hovered over him. The dark forms turned white and light blue. He closed his eyes, retreating to the darkness.

―――

The lighting was dim. James lay on his back in the hospital bed in a drug-induced haze. His right arm was hooked to an IV. His left arm was in a sling. Cool oxygen flowed into his nose from the nasal cannula. He moved his left arm and pain radiated from his shoulder.

James turned his head to his right. A curtain. He turned his head left and saw Anna sleeping on a nearby chair. She must've sensed him. She opened her eyes, then snapped upright in the chair, when she noticed that he was awake.

"James." She stood and approached the bedside, her eyes glassy.

"Anna." His voice was hoarse.

Anna pressed the "call" button for the nurse. She took his hand gently in hers. "How are you feeling?"

"My throat … is sore."

"I'll get you some water."

James squeezed her hand. "Don't go."

"I was so worried about you."

"I'm … sorry."

"For what?"

"For not … listening."

The overhead lights brightened. A nurse entered the hospital room, along with the doctor, a petite Indian woman. The nurse checked the medical equipment and his vital signs.

The doctor approached the bedside, holding a file.

Anna still stood on the opposite side of the bed, holding his hand.

"Hello, Mr. Harris. I'm Dr. Patel. How are you feeling?"

"My throat is … sore. My shoulder hurts," James replied.

"Your lungs were filled with water. You were on a respirator for two days. The endotracheal tube can cause some soreness, but that will dissipate over the next few days. We removed a bullet from your shoulder. You should retain full function after a few months of physical therapy. As for the pain, you have a button that you can push to increase the pain medication."

The nurse grabbed the remote, which was attached to a wire, and handed it to Anna. "He just has to push the red button."

"How did I get here?" James asked.

"Detectives Decker and Banks saved you," Anna said. "Decker pulled you out of the water. Banks resuscitated you."

"What about … Damon?"

"They arrested him."

FORTY-EIGHT
AWAKE

LATER THAT AFTERNOON, a nurse entered James's hospital room. "You have visitors. Detective Banks and Detective Decker."

James nodded, laying in his hospital bed. "Send them in."

Anna stood from her bedside chair. She met the detectives first, shaking their hands and thanking them for saving James's life.

"Would you mind if we spoke to him alone?" Detective Banks asked Anna.

"Of course not." She turned to James. "I'll be back."

James gave her a small smile of approval.

Anna grabbed her purse and left the hospital room.

Banks and Decker approached the bedside.

James pressed the control button, adjusting the bed so he was more upright.

"Good to see that you're awake," Banks said, smelling like cigarettes.

"It's good to be awake," James replied.

"Mind if we ask you a few questions?"

"Do you mind answering mine?"

Banks sat in the bedside chair and removed his notepad and pen from his pocket. "Depends on what they are."

"Fair enough."

"I'm recording, if that's okay?" Decker said as he tapped on his cell phone.

"That's fine," James replied.

Decker stood next to Banks, his phone in hand.

James took a deep breath. "Before we start, I'd like to thank you two for saving my life. So … *thank you*."

Decker nodded.

"I should've taken your theory more seriously," Detective Banks said. "I had tunnel vision."

"I appreciate that, but I think you were right to be skeptical," James replied. "Looking back now, it did sound crazy. Celebrity couples and all."

"Maybe, but you were right as rain."

"Why did you change your mind?"

"About looking into Damon?"

"Yes."

"You got me thinking about the case. That's how my mind works. If there's something unfinished, I can be obsessive. So I looked into Damon's financial records and found out that he had recently purchased a $55,000 truck with cash. That made me suspicious, so I called Decker." Banks gestured to his partner. "Decker was gonna go alone."

"Damon's house is on my way home," Detective Decker said.

"Luckily, I insisted on going with him," Banks said. "I had a bad feeling, and I didn't want my partner going without backup."

"What made you come to the quarry?" James asked.

"We didn't go to the quarry initially. We went to Damon's trailer. Saw your car on the road, Damon's truck in the driveway, but nobody was in the house. There's nothing around there except for the quarry, so I went to the quarry and Decker checked the trail."

"When I got to the cliff, I heard splashing. I looked over the edge, and I saw the water churning. I moved closer to the edge and I saw an arm flailing in the water. So I jumped." Decker stared through James for a moment. "If Rachel hadn't talked me into jumping off that cliff as a kid, I don't think I would've jumped."

James dipped his head. A wave of sadness washed over him. Even in death, Rachel had saved *him*, something James couldn't do for her when it mattered the most. James didn't believe Damon's claim that Rachel had manipulated him to kill James.

"As you probably know, we have Damon Williams in custody, but we're still gathering evidence," Detective Decker said. "We need to know exactly what happened when you went to his house three days ago. Start from the beginning. Why did you go to Damon's house? What was your plan?"

"I didn't want a confrontation," James replied. "I just wanted to look around. I figured he'd be at work on a Monday morning."

"You didn't hear?"

"Hear what?"

"Taylor Construction's out of business. They liquidated their trucks and equipment last month to pay off their creditors. It was ugly. The employees hadn't been paid. George Taylor had to step up so they didn't get stiffed."

"I should've known. Matt told me they were in trouble. That explains why Damon was home." James then told them about sneaking into Damon's backyard, and Damon pulling the gun on him and forcing him to the quarry ledge. "When we were walking on the trail through the woods, Damon told me that Rachel wanted Damon to kill me."

Banks jotted notes as James spoke.

Decker tilted his head, still holding his phone to record their conversation. "That doesn't make any sense."

James said, "Damon said that he and Rachel were in love and that Rachel convinced him I was abusing her and that she needed Damon to kill me so they could be together."

"Have you ever abused Rachel?" Decker asked with narrowed eyes.

James scowled at Decker. "*Never*. We've been through this before."

"Let's stay on task," Banks said. "What happened next?"

"I told Damon it was bullshit, that Rachel thought Damon was a loser."

"What did he say to that?" Banks asked.

"He agreed. He thought Rachel was manipulating him, but he found out and killed her instead of me."

"That doesn't make any sense," Decker said. "Sounds like Damon might be a delusional psychotic who was fixated on Rachel."

For the first time, James agreed with Detective Decker.

FORTY-NINE
ONE WEEK LATER ...

JAMES SAT IN THE WHEELCHAIR, his left arm still in a sling, waiting for someone to push him outside. He didn't need the wheelchair, but it was hospital policy.

Flowers in various stages of decay sat on the windowsill of his hospital room, mostly from colleagues at Lebanon Valley College and a few neighbors. As much as James appreciated the sentiments, the flowers wouldn't make the trip home. After all, they were already dead, the water postponing the inevitable.

Anna zipped up the rolling suitcase and set it upright. "All packed."

"Thank you for everything," James said.

Anna stepped to James, leaned over, and kissed him on the lips. "I love you."

"I love you too."

She sighed. "I'm so relieved this is over."

"It's not over yet. They still have to convict Damon. I'm worried it'll be a circus."

Detectives Decker and Banks entered the hospital room, wearing suits. Banks's jacket was unbuttoned, allowing room for his gut, whereas Decker's jacket was buttoned, concealing his athletic frame.

"Speak of the devil," James said to Anna.

Anna pivoted to the approaching detectives.

"Good morning, James, Anna," Detective Banks said.

"Good morning, Detectives," Anna replied.

Detective Decker and James greeted each other with silent nods.

"We have a pre–*welcome home* gift for you," Banks said with a grin, showing his tinted yellow teeth. "Two of them to be exact."

James raised his eyebrows.

"We searched Damon's house and found your coin collection—or at least some of it. It's in evidence right now, but, once his case is closed, we'll return it to you."

"And we fished Damon's gun out of the quarry," Decker added.

Damon had chucked the gun into the quarry when he had seen Banks running down the hill to the quarry shore.

Decker continued. "It's a match to the gun that killed Rachel and Quentin Henderson. Damon's going down for life."

"That's great news," Anna said.

James smiled. "That is great news."

"We have a rock-solid case," Banks said.

"Is he still blaming everything on Rachel?"

Banks grunted. "The ramblings of a delusional psychopath. There's no evidence that Rachel was involved."

FIFTY
CONTEXT

JAMES KNELT before the masked man, trembling, staring down the barrel of his handgun. The man removed his mask, but it wasn't a man. It was Rachel.

"Wake up, James. Wake up." The female voice sounded faint and ethereal, like it emanated from above.

His eyelids fluttered and opened. He took quick, shallow breaths. His heart pounded in his chest. James stared at Anna's face, hovering over him in the moonlight.

Then her voice was loud and clear. "James, you were having a nightmare."

James sat upright in bed, struggling, using only his right arm. "I'm sorry for waking you."

She sat back on her haunches. "I'm fine. Are *you* okay?"

James slipped out of bed, wearing a t-shirt and his sling. "I'm going to get something to drink."

"You need company?"

James leaned over and pecked her on the lips. "I'm okay. Go back to sleep."

James put on his pajama pants and went downstairs to the kitchen. He poured himself a glass of water from the countertop filter. As he sipped his water, he thought about the dream, and he thought about what Damon had said.

She wanted me to kill you.

James filled his water glass again, then walked to his office. He set his glass on his desk, using an unopened bill as a coaster. He flipped through his inbox atop his desk, digging to the bottom, finding his handwritten recreation of the dialogue he had heard on the night Rachel had been murdered.

James sat at the desk and reread the conversation between the Live Man and Rachel that he had heard in bits and pieces. Originally, James had filled in the blanks of what had been inaudible, guessing at what had been said, given the context at the time, underlining the added words.

After reading the conversation several times, he grabbed several sheets of paper from the desk drawer and rewrote the conversation between Rachel and Damon. He recreated the inaudible words, using the new context that Damon was the "Live Man," also making the assumption that Damon had been telling the truth about Rachel manipulating Damon to kill James, and furthermore taking into consideration that Damon had figured out her ruse.

As he rewrote the conversation, he used a separate paper to play with the dialogue, trying to find the most logical words to complete the partially inaudible sentences.

"Who are you right now?" Rachel asked. "You're scaring me."

"Shut up," Damon replied.

"You must think you're tough. I don't believe it." James rearranged Rachel's words to be, "You were a little rough. I don't appreciate it."

"I don't give a fuck."

"Stop pointing that at me. What's wrong with you? You're out of control."

"Now you notice me," Damon replied.

"If you kill me, I can't do what you say," Rachel said. James rearranged this sentence to be, "If you <u>want</u> me, <u>you</u> <u>will</u> do what <u>I</u> say," Rachel said.

Damon raised his voice. "You think I'm stupid, don't you?"

Rachel replied in a soothing voice. "<u>No</u>, <u>I</u> <u>don't</u>." Or maybe she replied, "<u>Of</u> <u>course</u> <u>not</u>."

"Bullshit. I know the truth," Damon said.

"<u>No</u>, <u>you</u> <u>don't</u>." James tried to remember the tone of her words. Rachel's voice had been soft at this point, so he changed this sentence to "<u>I</u> <u>love</u> <u>you</u>."

"Stop *lying*. You're <u>a</u> <u>fucking</u> <u>liar</u>."

"<u>I</u> <u>don't</u> <u>know</u> what you're talking about."

"Don't *lie*. <u>She</u> <u>told</u> me," Damon said.

"She doesn't know <u>what</u> <u>she's</u> <u>talking</u> <u>about</u>. She's <u>a</u> <u>liar</u>," Rachel replied.

These four lines of dialogue felt off to James for several reasons. He couldn't think of anytime that Rachel had used the word *liar*. She would say something more descriptive like the person was delusional or a gossip. Also, Rachel stating, "I don't know what you're talking about" in response to "You're a fucking liar" seems out of place. If Rachel's response is correct, Damon would have to make a more specific accusation. And Damon's reference to a *she* is odd. He likely knew very few women, and even less that he and Rachel both knew. That's when it hit him like a bolt of lightning. *Liv*.

James rewrote the four lines of dialogue.

"Stop *lying*. You're <u>having</u> <u>an</u> <u>affair</u>."

"<u>I</u> <u>don't</u> <u>know</u> what you're talking about."

"Don't *lie*. <u>Liv</u> <u>told</u> me," Damon said.

"She doesn't know <u>what</u> <u>she's</u> <u>talking</u> <u>about</u>. She's <u>a</u> <u>gossip</u>," Rachel replied.

The bedroom door shut. They were quiet for a while, then Rachel said, "Don't look at me like that."

"You don't <u>have</u> <u>the</u> power <u>anymore</u>," Damon replied.

James put the pieces together. He thought about Rachel coming home, smelling like cologne. He thought about their lack of a sex life. He thought about Damon's half-hearted attempts to find James during the home invasion, which would make sense, if he was supposed to kill James but had no intention of doing so.

Rachel wanted Damon to kill me, but she broke his heart, so he double-crossed her.

James rushed from his office to the downstairs bathroom. He flipped up the lid, dropped to his knees, and vomited the remnants of his dinner.

Light footsteps padded downstairs.

James spat and flushed the reddish-brown puke. He washed his mouth out in the sink.

Anna appeared in the bathroom doorway, as James dried his face with a towel. "Are you sick?"

James hung the towel on the rack and pivoted to Anna. "I think Rachel tried to have me killed."

Anna scrunched her face. "You don't believe Damon, do you?"

"I need to show you something."

Anna placed her hand on his hip. "I'm worried about you."

"I need to show you something," James repeated, leading Anna to his office. He explained that, shortly after Rachel was murdered, he had recreated a conversation between Damon and Rachel. Of course, he hadn't known it was Damon at the time. Then he explained how some of the words between them had been inaudible, so he had used context to fill in the blanks. However, now that the context had changed, he rewrote the conversation. "Read this," James said, handing Anna the written conversation.

Anna took the paper tentatively. She sat at James's desk, reading, while James read over her shoulder. Anna finished and swiveled in the chair to James.

"What do you think?" James asked.

"The parts that you underlined, you were guessing, right?"

"It's an educated guess."

"You could be wrong about what they said. Even the stuff you didn't guess. Memories aren't reliable, especially in stressful situations. Not to mention, Damon's a psychopath. Not exactly a reliable source."

"Damon might not be a reliable source, but I have a good memory." James hesitated for a moment. "Also, Rachel could be very kind and loving, but …"

"But what?" Anna asked.

"She could also be cold and calculating. I wanted to have children, but she didn't want to be burdened."

"Lots of people don't want to be burdened by children. Lots of *parents* don't want to be burdened by children. Rachel had a demanding career."

"But there wasn't any emotion behind it. It was calculated. *Kids are a pain. End of story.* Maybe that's the way she felt about me."

"I think you're being too hard on her."

James paced in the office, shaking his head.

"What?" Anna asked, still sitting in the swivel chair.

He stopped pacing and faced her. "It wasn't just me. She was the queen bee in school. Played with people for fun. Manipulated infatuated boys to do things for her. That's what she did to Damon."

Anna frowned. "According to him."

"No. That's what *Liv* told me."

"I don't know, James. I don't know."

James paced again, his speech rapid. "I think Rachel manipulated Damon to kill me. That's why she raised our life insurance policies to two million dollars. But Damon found out she was having an affair, so he double-crossed her—raped and killed her, took my coins, and sold them. The rape was about power. He wanted to take his power back from Rachel."

"You said *our* life insurance policies. She upped *her* life insurance policy too? Why not just yours?"

James stopped pacing and faced Anna again. "I think because it's less suspicious. If she only raised mine and I died, the cops might've had questions."

"If you're right, there's still a big question mark."

"I know. I've been thinking about that."

"And?"

James ran both hands though his disheveled hair. "I've been through all her stuff. There's no evidence of another man."

Anna stood from the swivel chair and took his hands. "The simplest explanation is usually correct. Maybe there wasn't another man. The police think Damon's a delusional psychopath and a liar, with a fixation on Rachel. Maybe they're right."

"I don't know." James closed his eyes, picturing Rachel's face. It was blurry. When he opened his eyes, he said, "I don't think I ever really knew her."

FIFTY-ONE
LEBANON COUNTY JAIL

TWO WEEKS LATER, James sat at a metal desk, dividers between him and the other visitors. A thick polycarbonate "glass" separated him from the prisoners. His underarms and lower back were sticky with sweat. The jail smelled like body odor and mold.

It had taken Detective Banks and the district attorney to arrange the meeting. Damon was in jail, still awaiting trial. He had been remanded to the county jail without bail. The defense attorney had recommended to Damon that he *not* take the meeting, but Damon had overruled his counsel.

Damon appeared behind the polycarbonate window. In perfect synchronicity, he and James picked up their receivers and pressed them to their ears. Damon said, "I had a feeling you'd come for a visit."

"Were you telling the truth about Rachel manipulating you to kill me?" James asked.

"Do you know how expensive everything is in here?" Damon asked.

"No."

Damon brushed his thin mustache with his thumb and index finger. "I could use some money in my commissary account."

James scowled. "How much?"

"Five hundred dollars."

"Fine. Were you telling the truth?"

Damon shrugged. "Who knows? Who the hell remembers everything they ever said?"

James gripped the receiver tight, his knuckles white. "Did Rachel want you to kill me?"

"Probably. You're a little bitch."

James clenched his jaw. He took a deep breath, trying not to let Damon get under his skin. "Was Rachel having an affair?"

Damon smirked. "I doubt she was satisfied with your little dick."

"Liv told you that Rachel was having an affair, didn't she?"

His face tightened for a split second. His smirk evaporated. "I don't know anything about that."

"That's why you killed Rachel, isn't it? You two were supposed to be together, but she was having an affair on *you*."

Damon glared through the polycarbonate.

"Who was the guy?"

Damon slammed the receiver on the base.

"Who was the guy?" James shouted.

Damon stood from the table and said, "Guard."

"Who was the guy?" James shouted again.

Damon disappeared with the guard.

James hung up the receiver and thought, *He believes there was an affair. That's for sure. But I don't think he knows who it was.*

FIFTY-TWO
NEXT SUMMER

ON A HUMID SUMMER DAY, James meandered between his rows of corn, picking pole beans that had used his cornstalks as support. As he picked beans, his mind drifted to the events of the past year. His meeting at the jail had been the last time he had seen Damon. James had never received the closure he desired. Either Rachel was a psychopath who had tried to have James killed, or she had been an innocent victim whom James had failed to protect. He didn't know which.

Damon had been convicted of double homicide and had been sentenced to life in prison, without the possibility of parole.

Anna had moved in with James six months ago. James suspected that Anna wanted a marriage proposal, but he had yet to propose. Their relationship was mostly amicable, although Anna accused him of holding back, of not letting her in completely. The truth was, James couldn't let go of Rachel. There wasn't a day that passed that he hadn't thought of her. James was convinced that Liv was the only one who really knew Rachel.

Three months ago, James and Anna had finally moved into the master bedroom. James had figured enough time had passed for whatever bad juju came from a murder to disappear. He had thought about selling the place, but he loved his house and garden, and he didn't think anyone would pay the market value, given what had happened in the master bedroom.

James's cell phone chimed, jarring him from his thoughts. He set down his basketful of beans, reached into his pocket, and grabbed his cell phone. He nearly swiped left on the unfamiliar number, thinking it might be a telemarketer, but changed his mind for no logical reason. "Hello?" James said.

"Is this James Harris?" the woman asked.

"Yes. May I ask who's calling?"

"This is Leah Henderson."

James was speechless for a beat. "Oh, ... hi, Leah. How are you?"

"I wasn't sure if I should call you. Sometimes I just wanna forget everything. You know what I mean?"

"Yes. I think I do."

"I said I'd call if I ever found anything, so I'm calling. This morning I was going through Quentin's things, finally throwing out some stuff, and I found a prepaid cell phone."

James hung on her every word.

"Are you still there?" she asked.

"I'm here," he replied.

"Well, I charged it and turned it on. There was hardly anything on it, except for a few texts."

"What did they say?"

"I think you should come over and see for yourself."

———

Leah opened her front door, the prepaid cell phone in hand. She wore shorts and a baggy t-shirt with no makeup. Her eyes were puffy and her hair was disheveled, with streaks of white.

"Thank you for calling me," James said.

"I want you to take this phone when you go," she said, holding out the phone. "I don't want anything to do with it."

James hesitated, then took the phone.

"There's a text string with a 717 number. I think Quentin is listed as *me*, assuming this is his phone."

"Did you try calling the 717 number?"

"No. I don't want anything to do with it."

Under the shade of Leah Henderson's front porch, James read the text conversation.

717-555-2771: Meet hitman on Sunday, 4-10, 1:00 a.m. Meet at the bottom of the driveway. Pull in far enough that your car can't be seen from the main road. Crack the safe in the husband's first floor office. Make sure the hitman does his job. DO NOT HARM RACHEL.

ME: I'm having second thoughts. I can crack the safe, but I don't want anything to do with a murder.

717-555-2771: Do as you're told, or I'll make sure you spend the rest of your life in prison. Don't forget. I'm sitting on a mountain of evidence against you.

ME: Do you know the hitman?

717-555-2771: He's solid. A friend of a friend.

ME: You don't know him?

717-555-2771: Do your fucking job and everything will be fine.

James looked up from the screen. "Is that it?"

"There's one more text," Leah said. "It looks like Quentin made a contact in the phone and sent it to himself."

James tapped to the main text screen, finding the other text string. He tapped on the text. It wasn't a string or a conversation though. It was a single text.

QH: I am being blackmailed into a burglary by Detective Frank Decker. I am tasked with cracking a safe, stealing a coin collection worth a half million dollars, and making sure the hitman kills the husband. I do NOT want to be involved with a murder, and I will NOT participate in the murder. For the record, I am only participating in the burglary under threat of incarceration by Decker.

FIFTY-THREE
NEED TO KNOW

AFTER MEETING WITH LEAH HENDERSON, James had called Detective Harvey Banks and set up an appointment to meet with him later that afternoon. Even though Decker was Banks's partner, James felt that he knew Banks well enough to believe he was an honest cop.

James sat across from Banks at his metal desk. The detective's cramped office was about the size of a prison cell.

Banks read through the text string on the prepaid cell phone. When he was done reading, he asked, "Did you try calling the phone number?"

"A recording says the number's unavailable," James replied.

Harvey nodded. "Even if this is authentic, Quentin's dead and Damon's in prison for life. There's nothing more we can do."

"Read the other text."

Banks tapped on the phone and read the other text, the one that implicated his partner. He exhaled heavily and set down the cell phone.

"Damon was telling the truth," James said. "Rachel convinced Damon to kill me, but Damon found out that Rachel was having an affair, so he killed Rachel in a fit of rage. Decker forced Quinten Henderson to steal my coins and to make sure Damon finished the job. Decker must've been the one having an affair with Rachel. He's involved in this."

Detective Banks frowned. "What evidence do you have to back up your story?"

"Damon told me that Rachel manipulated him to kill me."

"That's hearsay, not evidence. We investigated, and there was no evidence to back up that claim. *None.*"

"What about the texts? Quentin Henderson said Decker blackmailed him to crack my safe and to make sure Damon finished the job."

"More hearsay. Not to mention Quentin Henderson was a career criminal. Do you know how often criminals accuse cops of crime? Happens all the time." Banks held up the phone. "This isn't proof of anything. Quentin Henderson might've sent that text to himself to use as his defense in the event he was caught. It's simply a dead man's opinion at this point. And we're not even certain Quentin Henderson typed that text."

James gripped the armrests, his body taut. "Decker always had something against me. I thought you two were playing good-cop, bad-cop, but I think he was upset that Rachel was killed instead of me."

Banks held up his hand like a stop sign. "I'm gonna stop you right there, James. Detective Decker's a good cop. He's been my partner for ten years. I trust him with my life. Do I need to remind you that he saved *your* life? If I had been on that cliff, you would've drowned, because there's no way in hell I would've jumped."

James stood from his seat and snatched the prepaid cell phone from the desktop. "I'm assuming you won't do shit with this?"

Banks shook his head. "You're wrong about this. It's over. The case is closed."

"If you won't do your job, I will." James pivoted and left the office, leaving the door open in his wake. James left the police station parking lot unnecessarily fast, chirping his front tires in the process.

On the way home, James squeezed the steering wheel, his knuckles white. He pictured Frank Decker and Rachel having sex in their bed. He imagined them plotting to kill him. His cell phone chimed in the center cupholder. James glanced at his phone but didn't answer.

James parked in his garage, next to Anna's Toyota Camry. He exited his Honda and left the garage. He slipped off his shoes in the mudroom, then went inside. The smell of cooking burgers and baked eggplant wafted into his nostrils.

Anna stood at the stovetop, tending the burgers. She glanced over her shoulder. "Hey. I tried to call you."

James trudged into the kitchen and leaned against the center island, facing Anna. He told Anna about his meeting with Leah Henderson and his subsequent meeting with Detective Banks.

"I wish you would've told me," Anna said. "I could've gone with you."

James glowered at Anna. "Did you hear what I said? Decker's involved. He was having an affair with Rachel. He blackmailed Quentin Henderson."

Anna turned off the burner and set the pan of burgers on the quartz countertop. She faced James. "Maybe. But you don't know that for certain. Detective Banks is right. There's no real evidence to corroborate what Damon said or what Quentin Henderson texted. And there's no evidence that Rachel was having an affair."

James hung his head. "You sound like Banks."

Anna stepped closer, taking his hands in hers. "I'm not trying to. I know this has been incredibly hard for you. I feel like you've been holding on so tight to Rachel because you feel so much guilt for what happened."

James's vision blurred with his tears. "I need to know what happened."

"I know. But you may never know, and you still have to live your life. I feel like we've had this cloud over us during our entire relationship. I think it's time to let go. None of this was your fault."

James thought about Rachel. They had been together for fifteen years. He wiped the corners of his eyes. Anna hugged him, squeezing tight. James was stiff at first, but then reciprocated.

Anna tilted her head up and said, "I just want you to be happy. I want us to be happy together. I want us to move forward *together*."

"So do I."

FIFTY-FOUR
THE HARD TRUTH

THE FOLLOWING MONDAY EVENING, James sat on a plastic chair in a back room of the Lebanon Public Library. Survivors of violent crime and their families were arranged in a tight circle.

"James?" Anna asked from across the circle. "Would you like to share?" She always asked, and James always declined.

This time James said, "Okay."

Everyone stared at James expectantly.

James stared at his hands and said, "My stepfather used to beat me, when I was a kid. It started as soon as my mom and I moved into his house, when I was six, and it didn't stop until I left his house at eighteen. He beat me for anything or nothing. I was a good kid. I did my chores. Got good grades. I was well-mannered. But it was never enough." James raised his gaze, focusing on Anna. "He always found a reason to beat me. I never stood up for myself. I never even considered standing up for myself. I used to freeze. It was almost like an out-of-body experience. My mind took me away from what was happening to me. I think it was my mind's way of protecting myself."

Many of the women in the group nodded along with James's story.

"Twenty-two years after I left my stepfather's house, I was married, with a house of my own and a great job. I thought I was happy. I thought I had left it all behind. Then two men broke into our house. I was sleeping in the guest bedroom because my wife and I had had a fight. I heard the men talking through the vent. The house had a crawl space that connected the rooms. I thought I could go through the crawl space and pull her inside with me, so we could hide together, but I took too long. The men got there before me."

He sniffed and paused, trying to control his emotions. "I could've opened the crawl-space door and helped her, but I was afraid. I froze, just like I did when I was a kid." His voice wavered as he said, "I hid like a coward, while one of the men raped and murdered my wife. I can still hear her crying for help, calling my name." James wiped the corners of his eyes with his index fingers, trying to stop the tears at the source.

The room was dead quiet for a minute, while James regained his faculties.

James took a deep breath. "I don't think I ever really knew my wife. She might've been …" James trailed off, not wanting to reveal his suspicions about Rachel to the group. "My wife was raped and murdered. I could've helped her, but I did *nothing*. That's the truth."

FIFTY-FIVE
SCI FRACKVILLE

ELEVEN DAYS LATER, James went to the State Correctional Institution at Frackville in Schuylkill County, Pennsylvania.

The visiting room was filled with perfectly spaced stainless-steel tables with attached stainless-steel disks that functioned as the most uncomfortable seats ever created. A few vending machines lined the walls with overpriced snacks and soda. Corrections officers patrolled the room, making sure no one touched or acted inappropriately or aggressively.

Damon wore a brown smock and matching brown pants. He sat at the stainless-steel table across from James. James had been surprised that Damon had agreed to add him to his list of approved visitors. James figured Damon didn't receive many, if any, visitors. Plus, James had added five hundred dollars to Damon's commissary account, as payment for the meeting.

Damon had a faded black eye and bruising around his neck. He lifted his chin to James. "Thanks for the commissary."

"No problem," James replied.

"What do you want?"

"I had some questions to ask you. You told me that Rachel was manipulating you. How did you know?"

"Liv. She knew I was in love with Rachel. I think she didn't want me to get hurt. I thought Rachel loved me, but I was just a pawn." He whispered the next part so the guards couldn't hear. "Bitch got what she deserved. Didn't she?"

James clenched his fists under the table, unsure why he still gave a shit about Rachel. "Did Liv tell you who Rachel was having an affair with?"

"No. I asked her, but she wouldn't tell me. Said it wasn't important. Liv was always looking out for me. Since we were kids."

"I'm sorry for your loss," James replied, referring to her suicide.

Damon sniffed. "I still don't believe it. Liv never would've committed suicide." Damon whispered, "I think someone shoved those pills down her throat, then cut her wrists."

James leaned forward, his brow furrowed. "Who?"

"I think whoever sent that guy to crack your safe. When shit went sideways, they were probably worried about loose ends. Rachel told Liv everything. Maybe they thought Liv was a loose end."

"Did Liv know that Rachel wanted to kill me?"

"I doubt it, but Liv knew who the mystery man was. Figure that out, and you got Liv's murderer."

James glanced around, making sure no one was listening. Then he whispered, "What about Frank Decker?"

Damon raised one side of his mouth in contempt. "Could be. I always hated that motherfucker. He would have access to a burglar with the skills to crack a safe. He could've easily staged Liv's suicide. I bet he investigated her death too."

James whispered, "Before Liv died, she sent me a message, saying that she wanted to talk to me about something important, but she didn't want to talk on the phone. Maybe she was planning to tell me that Rachel was having an affair with Decker. Decker definitely knew that Liv was Rachel's best friend and confidante. Like you said, maybe he thought Liv was a loose end, that she knew too much. Maybe Decker went to see her, to find out what she knew, and …"

Damon shook his head, a scowl on his face. "I bet it *was* him. If I was out, I'd kill that piece of shit myself."

They didn't speak for a long time, sitting with the revelation.

James broke the silence. "Do you think it was Decker's idea to kill me?"

"I don't think so," Damon replied. "Rachel was the puppet master."

"Why didn't you just walk away?"

"From Rachel?"

James nodded.

Damon shrugged. "I was tired of being treated like nothing. My whole life, the game's been rigged against me. I decided to flip the board over and play by my own rules for once."

James wondered if Rachel and Decker had been perfect for each other.

FIFTY-SIX
THE PHENOM

TREE BRANCHES SCRATCHED HIS CAR, as James parked on the grassy roadside. The rural neighborhood featured irregular lots of one to six acres in size, separated by forest. Two mailboxes were visible from James's windshield. One was roughly forty yards away; the other was one hundred yards away. The name on the farthest mailbox read Decker.

James had purchased a background check on Frank Decker and had found his home address. With Google Earth, James had searched Decker's property, using the information to plan his approach. From James's previous involvement with Banks and Decker, he had guessed that they worked the day shift, between 8:00 a.m. and 4:00 p.m., although they often worked well past four. James glanced at the time on his dashboard—*7:26 a.m.*

About fifteen minutes later, Detective Decker's SUV appeared. He turned right onto the main road and drove away. James exited his Honda and cut through the woods toward Decker's house. Morning sunlight filtered through the tree canopy. Robins chirped overhead. Squirrels scampered about.

He thought about the steps he had taken not to leave any DNA at the scene. Earlier that morning, Anna had asked him why he was obsessively lint brushing his clothes. James hadn't had a good answer, so he'd said, "I don't know." Anna had been too busy getting ready for work to be suspicious.

James stopped at the forest edge, peering over the raspberry brambles at Decker's redbrick rambler. Roughly one-quarter acre of his lot was cleared to accommodate the small house and the green grass. James scanned the house for any signs to indicate an alarm system but found none.

He slipped through the brambles, the thorns catching on his jeans and his gloves. Before he neared the house, he slipped booties over his shoes and a hairnet over his head. James checked the front door and several front windows. They were all locked. He crept around the house to the back patio. A hot tub gurgled in the corner. James imagined Rachel and Decker in the hot tub together. He checked the sliding glass door, yanking on the handle harder than necessary. Also locked.

He noticed that one corner of the patio had a short concrete-block retaining wall. James grabbed a heavy concrete block from the retaining wall and carried it to the sliding glass door. He looked around, suddenly feeling like someone was watching him, but all he saw was the surrounding forest. He twisted and heaved the stone. The sliding glass door shattered into a thousand pieces.

James expected an alarm to blare, but nothing happened. He entered Decker's house. The kitchen appeared newer than the house, with stainless-steel appliances and granite counters. James went through drawers and cabinets but found nothing interesting. Lots of protein powders, energy drinks, eggs, and meat.

James stepped into the living room, which was nicely appointed with wood floors, black leather furniture, and a massive flat-screen television. The door to the basement was open. James descended the steps. The basement was a man cave with another massive television, more leather couches, a wet bar, and various sports and alcohol memorabilia hanging from the walls.

A trophy case commemorated Frank Decker's high school sports career. A framed picture from the *Lebanon Chronicle* showed a young Frank Decker, smiling, wearing shoulder pads, a baseball bat in one hand and a basketball in the other. The headline read "Phenom." Another frame featured a team picture, the boys wearing their jerseys and football pants, sitting in neat rows on the metal bleachers. The coaches wore red polos and khakis. *West Lebanon High School Football, 2004 State Champs* was printed across the bottom of the image.

He left the trophy case and checked behind the bar, noting the plethora of whiskeys. The fridge was stocked with beer.

James left the basement and returned to the living room. He followed the hallway to the master bedroom at the end of the hall, passing an office and a guest bedroom on the way. James rifled through Decker's drawers, finding nothing interesting. He searched the closet too and under the bed, but still found nothing except for a Glock handgun and three boxes of hollow-point nine-millimeter ammunition.

After the master bedroom, James checked the master bathroom. He found some prescribed antidepressants and some Viagra tablets behind the mirror. James wondered if Decker took them for need or for fun. Rachel had once suggested getting some Viagra to boost their sexual experience, but James had been afraid of an ER visit for an endless erection.

James left the master bathroom and bedroom. He walked down the hall and checked the guest bedroom. The room was dusty and appeared to be rarely used. He proceeded to the office. A cherrywood desk dominated the room, with bookshelves lining one wall. A laptop and a stack of bills sat on the desktop. James opened the laptop. As the computer loaded, he searched the desk drawers. Nothing but office supplies and an ornate pocketknife.

The computer finished loading. James was surprised there was no password request. James sat at Decker's desk, surfing on his laptop, checking the word files, the videos, the audio files, and his internet browsing history. Nothing was out of the ordinary, except for his extensive porn addiction, which wasn't that out of the ordinary anymore. James stared at the box of tissues on the desk and sprang from his seat, realizing that Decker likely masturbated in that very seat.

James thought, *If Decker was having an affair with Rachel, he would've kept something of hers. Someone who watches that much porn would want video of himself and Rachel.* James thought about Rachel's adventurous sexual exploits, nearly certain she would've acquiesced. *He might've thrown everything away when Rachel was murdered. Maybe. But, if he had feelings for Rachel, he would want to relive those memories. And, if he's not a suspect, he wouldn't be concerned about keeping the videos, provided they existed in the first place. But where would he keep them?*

James searched the desk drawers again, doing a more thorough search this time, figuring the most logical place to keep the video footage would be near the laptop and Decker's likely masturbation location. He found two flash drives inside a box of pens.

He inserted the flash drives into the USB ports on Decker's laptop. Then James navigated to the first flash drive, opening it. There was a single folder entitled Rachel. James double-clicked on the folder. Thumbnails for at least one hundred videos appeared. Their titles were self-explanatory. Three holes one night. Fuck in the woods. I cum on her face. Fuck in the shower. Acrobatic sex. She likes it rough. Fuck in the hot tub. Almost caught by my neighbor. Tied up. Whips and chains. Better than her hubby.

With a shaky finger, James double-clicked *Better than her hubby*. James watched Decker have sex with Rachel in several different positions. Rachel moaned and screamed, as Decker prodded her to tell him how much better he was than her husband.

"Your cock is so much bigger than my husband's," Rachel said between moans of ecstasy. "You fuck so much better. Keep going. Keep going."

During the rough sex, Decker often said, "This is my pussy now."

To which Rachel dutifully replied, "This is your pussy."

James shut the laptop, feeling nauseated but not wanting to

spew DNA on Decker's floor. After his stomach settled, James opened the laptop and checked the second flash drive. The video thumbnails appeared identical to the first flash drive. James figured Decker valued the videos enough that he worried about a flash drive failing, hence the backup. James shoved both flash drives into his pocket.

James paced in the office, taking deep breaths, his mind replaying the images he had just seen. He spoke aloud to himself. "Why do I give a shit? She probably tried to have me killed."

In a rage, he grabbed the laptop and flung it across the room. It hit the wall and dropped to the floor, seemingly still in one piece. James opened the top desk drawer and dumped the contents on the floor. The pocketknife landed on his shoe. He inspected the folded knife. It was beautiful. He grabbed the pocketknife and studied the sterling silver frame, which was inlaid with what resembled ivory. The one-hand button lock and the thumb stud were set with diamonds. James grabbed a bill from the desktop, removing a single sheet of paper from the envelope. He opened the blade and sliced the paper from end to end like a hot knife through butter. James wondered if it was Damascus steel.

James took the knife to the living room and gutted the leather couches, laughing as he went. Then he inspected the massive television on the wall. He smiled to himself, shut the knife, and slipped it into his pocket. He went to the television, reached up, grabbed the top edge, and hung on the screen.

The bracket snapped, and the TV fell face down, the screen shattering. James ran downstairs to the man cave, giggling like a maniac. He yanked the television off the wall and gutted the couches, like he'd done upstairs. When he shut the knife, he noticed a tiny inscription on the handle. It read, *Love always, RT*. James thought, *Rachel Taylor*. In a rage, James wound up and threw the knife at the mirror behind the bar, but he missed the mark, hitting the wall above the refrigerator, the knife dropping behind the appliance.

James exhaled and went to the bar. Baroque whiskey bottles

were prominently displayed behind the bar on shelves. James grabbed two bottles from the shelves and chucked them against the wall. One shattered; the other hit the wall with a *thud* and dropped to the floor, intact. James went to the wall and retrieved the indestructible whiskey bottle. He held the globular whiskey bottle, as he approached Decker's trophy case. Images of Decker and Rachel haunted him. He reared back and threw a fastball. The whiskey bottle shattered the glass door on the case.

James reached into the case and removed the framed photo with Decker's "Phenom" article. He opened the back of the frame, removed the old article, and ripped it to shreds, letting the old newspaper float to the floor. The framed team football picture still sat upright in the case. James grabbed the frame, intent on destroying another memento, but someone caught his eye.

A dark-skinned man sitting in the back row. One of the coaches. *Detective Banks.* James inspected the photo, staring at each face. He found Decker, his jawline rounder and his face as smooth as a baby's behind, but it was Decker. James almost missed the boy next to Decker. He was thinner and cheesing for the camera, but he was certain that it was Matt Taylor, his drunk ex-brother-in-law.

James tossed aside the framed image and went back upstairs to the kitchen. He opened the refrigerator. *Meatheads and their protein.* James removed the egg containers. Four dozen eggs in total. He chucked them around the house haphazardly, enjoying the *splats.*

He exited the hole where the sliding glass door used to reside. He grabbed the outdoor hose, pulled it to the middle of the living room, and removed the nozzle so the water would flow freely. On his way out, he turned the hose on full blast.

FIFTY-SEVEN
SEVEN HOURS IN HELL

BY LATE AFTERNOON, James was numb to Rachel's moans and gyrations, numb to Decker's big pecker, numb to the degradations that Rachel seemed to enjoy. He had been watching the videos for seven hours, searching for anything that might tie Decker to the murder or the burglary.

A hand touched James's shoulder, causing him to startle. He shut his laptop reflexively, turned to Anna, and removed his headphones.

Anna narrowed her eyes. "What are you doing?"

James rubbed his itchy eyes.

"You look terrible."

"I, *uh*, … I guess I should show you."

"Show me what?"

James opened his laptop.

"Were you watching porn?" Anna asked.

James handed her the headphones. "If you want audio?"

She scrunched her nose in disgust. "I'd rather not see this."

"You should." James pressed Play.

Anna and James watched Rachel's face on the screen, Decker behind her, pumping like a piston.

Anna put her hand to her mouth. "Oh, my god. That's Rachel."

James nodded.

Her voice trembled. "Is that you? Why would you show me this?"

James shook his head. "Watch."

They switched positions, and Decker peered into the camera lens.

"That's Detective Decker!" Anna said.

James stopped the video.

"Where did you get this?"

James swiveled in his chair to face Anna. "I shouldn't tell you. I don't want you to have to lie in the future."

Her eyes widened. "What did you do?"

James didn't reply.

"You broke into his house, didn't you?"

James didn't reply.

"You could go to prison."

James ran his hand through his disheveled hair. "You know how Banks said there wasn't enough evidence to look into Decker?"

"What does that have to do with anything?"

"There's not enough evidence to look into me either."

"If you stole this from Decker's house, you can't use this in court."

James hung his head. "It doesn't matter. Nothing on these videos tie him to the murder anyway. It's not against the law to fuck another man's wife."

FIFTY-EIGHT
INTRUDER

OVER THE NEXT WEEK, James had been jumpy, worried that the police would pay him a visit. He had racked his brain, thinking of a way to gather the evidence needed to connect Decker to the murder and to the burglary. Deep in his bones, James knew Decker was involved. However, James was out of ideas. The break-in of Decker's house had been James's Hail Mary play.

Anna had said, "You may never know what happened." As the days passed, James grew closer to accepting Anna's statement.

On Friday night, James and Anna had gone to bed around 10:30 p.m. It was the first night in a week that he hadn't thought about Frank Decker and Rachel.

James had been in a deep sleep when he'd been shaken. He opened his eyes.

Anna hovered over him, her face taut. "I think someone's in the house."

It took a moment to process her words. "What?"

She spoke in a harsh whisper. "Someone's in the house."

His initial thought was that it was the wind, but then he worried about the police—or Decker. But James had been so careful not to leave his DNA at Decker's house. Hadn't he? "Are you sure it wasn't the wind or the house settling?"

"I don't know."

James slipped out of bed and whispered back, "I'll check it out. If you hear anything, call the police."

Anna slipped out of bed. "I'm coming with you."

James grabbed her by the shoulders. "No. I can't let it happen again."

Anna nodded. "Be careful."

James grabbed the aluminum bat they kept by their bedside and exited the master bedroom. He crept down the hallway toward the top of the stairs. The second step creaked, sending a jolt of adrenaline through James's body. He stepped into the guest bedroom near the top of the stairs and hid against the wall, next to the open doorway. His intent was to wait and ambush whoever was coming.

His hands were hot and sweaty as he gripped the bat. The intruder's steps were slow and barely audible. Someone trying to be quiet. As the intruder neared the top of the stairs, his ragged breath was audible. The intruder snuck past the open doorway of the guest bedroom. James saw a stocky person, likely a man, dressed in all black, his head covered.

James slipped out of the guest bedroom. He took three quick steps and slammed the aluminum bat into the back of the man's skull. The intruder grunted and fell to the floor, dropping his handgun. James wound up and swung again, connecting with the guy's back, causing an audible *crack*. James swung repeatedly at the intruder's back in a rage. The intruder wasn't moving.

"James!" Anna shouted.

James dropped his bat, his chest heaving.

Anna padded toward the scene, from the bedroom. "He's not moving."

James gaped at the intruder, lying face down in his hallway. His back moved up and down slightly. "He's still alive."

Anna grabbed the gun from the floor. She aimed it at the

man, her finger straight and off the trigger. "Turn him over. If he tries anything, I'll shoot him." Before she'd met James, Anna had taken several courses on basic firearm safety and marksmanship.

In the adrenaline of the fight, James thought the man was Decker, but, as he turned over the intruder, he realized he was wrong. The man was too overweight to be Decker. James's stomach lurched as he removed the man's balaclava. "*Matt?*" James said. "What the *hell?*"

Matt wheezed. "Fuck ... you." He coughed up dark blood. Alcohol emanated from his pores.

"He needs an ambulance," Anna said.

"Did you call the police?" James asked, his tone frantic.

"They're on their way. Maybe I should call them back, let them know he's seriously injured?"

"Good idea."

Anna ran back to the master bedroom, taking the gun with her.

James knelt next to his former brother-in-law. "God *damn it*, Matt. What the *hell* are you doing here?"

"Got nothing ... to lose," Matt said, in between shallow wheezy breaths.

James assumed he was referring to the failed family business. "That's *bullshit*. You have Michelle and your boys."

Dark blood surrounded his mouth and stained his teeth. "They're ... gone. Divorce."

Anna's voice carried from the master bedroom, but her words were inaudible. She was likely on the phone with a 9-1-1 operator.

"Did you hire Damon to kill me?" James asked.

Matt coughed, spitting up more dark blood. "You ... did ... to kill ... Rachel."

"What the hell are you talking about?"

He wheezed, desperately seeking oxygen. "Frank ... told ... me."

Anna returned from the master bedroom, her cell phone in

hand. "An ambulance is coming too. They should be here any minute.

Matt's wheezing intensified. His body convulsed, as if he had been electrocuted.

James gaped at him, frozen like a deer in headlights.

"I think he's going into shock," Anna said.

Matt's body went limp. He stopped breathing.

James deadpanned, "I think he's dead."

FIFTY-NINE
THE BOX ... AGAIN

JAMES SAT at a metal table across from Detective Banks. James wondered if Detective Decker watched them through the two-way mirror.

Detective Banks glared at James. "You're telling me that Matt Taylor told you that Decker told him to kill you?"

James shook his head and glared back. "You're not listening. I asked Matt if he hired Damon to kill me. He said, *No, you did to kill Rachel*. I asked him what the hell he was talking about. That's when he said, *Frank told me*."

"That's it? *Frank told me*?"

"Yes."

"Did Anna hear Matt say this?"

"No. She was calling 9-1-1 at the time."

"I see a pattern. Someone ends up dead in your house, and you blame Detective Decker."

James crossed his arms over his chest. "Don't you see? Decker must've told Matt that I hired Damon to kill Rachel. Matt gets wasted one night and comes over to settle the score."

"How do you know Matt was drunk?"

"I could smell the alcohol on him."

Detective Banks leaned back in his chair, rubbing the gray

stubble on his chin. "Why do you have such a hard-on for Detective Decker?"

James clenched his jaw, knowing he couldn't mention the videos of Decker and Rachel. "He's involved. I know it."

"We'll see. We'll do a thorough investigation, and we'll see."

"I won't hold my fucking breath."

Banks leaned forward and placed his elbows on the table. He glowered at James. "You got something to say to me?"

James glowered back. "I gave you a cell phone implicating your partner, yet you did nothing."

"That cell phone didn't prove a thing."

"What about this?"

"Like I said, we'll see."

SIXTY
DETECTIVE BANKS

DETECTIVE HARVEY BANKS parked in front of a redbrick rambler with a cigarette between his lips. Errant leaves swirled in the wind. The surrounding trees were in their October glory, with bright yellow and red foliage. Banks exited his SUV. He took a final drag from his Newport, dropped the lit cigarette on the driveway, and mashed it into the macadam with his sneaker. Then he stepped to the front door.

Frank Decker opened the door before Banks had the opportunity to knock. Banks had texted, so the visit was expected.

Decker moved aside. "Come in."

Banks wiped his feet on the welcome mat before stepping inside. The interior smelled faintly of mold, despite what appeared to be new furniture in the living room. "New couch?"

"Some bitch spilled red wine on the old one."

Banks nodded.

"You want a beer?" Decker asked, changing the subject.

"Yeah, sure," Banks replied, following Decker into the kitchen.

Decker grabbed two beers from the fridge, opened them with a bottle opener, and handed one to Banks.

"Thanks," Banks said.

Banks wore jeans and a Philadelphia Eagles sweatshirt. They sat at the round kitchen table.

Decker took a long swig from his beer, set down the bottle, and said, "I have to admit, your message has me a little worried."

Banks nodded, his mouth turned down. "You should be worried."

Decker's eyes bulged.

"Chief Tannehill's opening an investigation on you. You'll be suspended tomorrow."

"Suspension? An investigation? For what?"

"James Harris is still convinced you had something to do with his wife's death."

Decker frowned. "The case is closed. There's nothing to investigate."

"He also thinks you had something to do with Matt Taylor, Olivia Wallace, and Quentin Henderson."

Decker sat upright, his body rigid. "That's *bullshit*. There's no evidence for any of that."

Banks took a drink from his beer, then set it on the table. "There's evidence. Witnesses. Text messages. Video footage—"

"Video footage?" Decker asked, incredulous. "Of what?"

"Can't say. Not sure if there's enough for a conviction, but there's enough for a trial."

"*Shit*. I can't believe Tannehill would pull this bullshit. Are you heading the investigation?"

"I convinced Tannehill to give me the case. It helps that I have a good rapport with Harris. I'd like to help you, make sure this investigation never goes to trial, but I won't do that if you're responsible for murder."

"I'm not. I promise you."

Banks narrowed his eyes. "The evidence says otherwise. You could be charged as an accomplice to felony murder."

Decker winced as if he'd been punched. His voice wavered. "I didn't do this. You have to believe me."

Banks leaned forward, resting his elbows on the table. "As

your friend, I do. As a detective, I need evidence. I need to know everything."

Decker hung his head. "I didn't kill anyone, but I did some things …"

"If I'm gonna put my ass on the line, I need to know the truth."

Decker chugged the rest of his beer and set down the empty bottle. He shook his head. "I'd rather not put you in the position of lying for me."

"You remember that fucking pedo we arrested your first year as a detective?" Banks asked. "Tyler Winters."

"After what he did to the Killinger girl, how could I forget?"

"Poor thing was so traumatized, we couldn't get her to pick him out of the lineup."

Decker grunted. "It was a fucking nightmare. No way she would've been able to handle a trial."

Banks nodded. "DA Ellis would've dropped the case like a hot potato."

Decker nodded. "He would've, if we hadn't pressed Winters."

"*We*? That was all you."

"That fucking perv had it coming." Decker took a deep breath. "I remember what you did for me. Going out on a limb, like you did."

Decker had entered Tyler's house without a search warrant and had scared the shit out of him, intimidating him into admitting he had molested the Killinger girl. Banks had been against the cowboy tactic and had waited outside. Of course, Tyler had recanted his confession, but Banks had corroborated Decker's story that the confession wasn't coerced. With Decker and Banks's testimony, the jury had convicted Tyler Winters. Had Banks told the truth, Decker would've likely been stripped of his detective shield, and Tyler Winters would've walked.

"I still have your back," Banks said, "but you gotta trust me. You gotta tell me the truth."

Decker stared at his hands for a long moment.

Banks stayed silent.

Decker finally raised his gaze and said, "I was in a relationship with Rachel. James Harris was abusing her. You know she had old bruising when she died. She showed me others months before. I wanted to arrest him, but she begged me not to. Said it would make things worse. I've seen enough DV cases to know she was probably right. She said she had a plan for us to be together. Convinced me to trust her. It killed me not to be able to protect her."

"What about Damon? He claims that Rachel manipulated him to kill James. Is that true?"

Decker leaned back in his chair, silent for several seconds. "It wasn't my idea. I didn't want anything to do with it, but I understood her desperation."

"Damon's telling the truth, isn't he?"

Decker nodded again. "I didn't know it was Damon. All I knew is that Rachel had someone to take care of James. My only involvement was Quentin. She needed someone to crack the safe, to make it look like a burglary gone wrong. She also wanted a second guy in case Damon fucked it up or needed backup." Decker hung his head. "We see DV victims all the time. They never get out. This was Rachel's chance to get out clean. I never thought …"

"How did you get Quentin to crack that safe?"

Decker hesitated for a second. "He owed me a favor."

"What kind of favor?"

"The kind that keeps a man out of prison."

"You coerced him? Threatened him with prison time?"

Decker stared at his hands again. "I'm not proud of it."

"What about Liv?" Banks asked.

Decker raised his gaze again. "What about her? She committed suicide. We worked the scene together. You know I didn't have anything to do with it."

"And Matt?"

Decker blew out a tired breath. "We were drinking together on the night he was killed. I let a few things slip. Told him that James had been abusing Rachel."

Banks arched his eyebrows. "Is that it?"

Decker wrung his hands. "I told him that I thought James hired Damon to kill Rachel, gave him the coin collection as payment."

"*Jesus*, Frank. There's no evidence of that." Banks chugged the rest of his beer, then set the bottle down unnecessarily hard. "If you were Joe fucking Schmo, telling Matt what you did would just be some blowhard talking shit. But you're a detective, working on his sister's case. You have credibility. When you told Matt that James was beating Rachel, that he hired the man who killed her, you set him on the path to his own death. Do you realize that?"

Decker fidgeted in his seat. "I know."

"Is that it?"

Decker showed his palms. "That's it. I swear. Can you help me?"

"You're lucky Quentin Henderson's not alive to testify."

"I know."

Banks stood from the table. "We can't talk anymore. I have to maintain the illusion of objectivity."

Decker stood too. "I understand. I'm sorry for … everything. You're about to retire. This is the last thing you need."

Banks nodded.

Decker followed Banks to the front door.

Banks opened the door and turned to his friend. "You're a good cop, Frank. It'll blow over." Banks extended his hand to shake, but Decker hugged him instead.

When they separated, Decker's eyes were glassy. "Thank you. If you ever get in a jam in the future, I'll be there. No questions asked."

"I know you will." Banks left the redbrick rambler. As he drove away from the house, Detective Harvey Banks spoke into the microphone hidden beneath his sweatshirt. "Arrest him."

SIXTY-ONE
DUMB LUCK

JAMES PACED in front of his afternoon criminology class. "There's a book, *Ordinary Men* by Christopher Browning. It's about a German reserve police battalion during World War II. Many of these men were older reservists and civilians. Most of these men didn't grow up in the Hitler Youth. They weren't Nazi true believers. As the title suggests, they were ordinary men.

"They were sent to Poland to maintain law and order, after the German army conquered the country. The Nazis viewed the Jews as a fifth column, actively working against their war effort. So, the first thing they did was round up all the Jewish men between the ages of eighteen and sixty-five, and they sent them away on trains."

James scanned his classroom, checking that his audience was engaged. They were. He had a class size of roughly forty-five. Most of his students were in their late-teens and early twenties.

"Over time, their orders changed from arrests and train rides to executions. They took thousands of civilians, including women and children, into the woods and shot them. Their commander didn't like their mission. He gave his troops the opportunity to go home. Nobody had to participate in these mass murders. But they did. In fact, the vast majority of these men participated in the mass murders." James paused for effect. "Why? Were they evil?"

The rear classroom door opened. Detective Banks slipped into a seat in the back.

James said, "Many of these men stated some form of responsibility as a motive. They didn't want to shirk their duty, figuring that someone else would have to do it if they didn't. Deference to authority also played a part. Think about what we covered last class. Stanley Milgram's experiment taught us that nearly two-thirds of people will electrocute someone to death simply because someone in a lab coat tells them to do so."

James made eye contact with several students as he spoke. "At first, the men in this German police battalion were sickened by the brutal orders they were given. They struggled to do their duty. But, over time, it became easier and easier. Many men grew to enjoy their work. They *enjoyed* the killing. In our comfortable surroundings, it's easy for us to think that we would never do such a thing. It's easy to think that we would've opposed the Nazis. Of course, for most of us, that's untrue. Under the dark spell of authority, we would likely conform and commit the worst atrocities you can imagine. If we truly want to be men and women of courage, we must understand the lessons of history. We must understand the dangers of being possessed by our ideologies. Most important, we must understand the darker side of human nature. In the *Gulag Archipelago*, Aleksandr Solzhenitsyn wrote, *The line dividing good and evil cuts through the heart of every human being*."

A student raised her hand.

James pointed to her and said, "Yes, Ashley."

"It's always men who do these terrible things," Ashley said. "Why can't we teach men to be nonviolent?"

"You're fighting three hundred thousand years of Homo sapien evolution, six million years of evolution if you count our ancestors. I don't know if nonviolence is the answer, although I believe violence should be a last resort. We will always have bullies. We will always have criminals. We will always have tyrannical governments. What we need more than ever are strong men and women who are virtuous and courageous. Otherwise, the evil inherent in all of us will win."

James glanced at his watch. "We'll pick this up on Monday. Have a great weekend."

The students collected their laptops and backpacks and filed out of the classroom. Detective Banks approached James. They met on the carpet, in front of the built-in student desks.

"I enjoyed your lecture," Banks said.

"Thanks. What can I do for you?" James asked.

"I wanted to let you know that Decker didn't make bail."

James tilted his head. "That's surprising. Conspiracy to commit burglary isn't usually a charge where a judge would deny bail."

Despite James and Damon accusing Frank Decker of murdering Liv, their evidence was circumstantial at best, so no murder charge was considered by the district attorney. The only evidence they had was Decker's recorded confession to Banks, and the only crimes he admitted to were conspiracy to commit burglary and extortion. At least that's what James had thought.

"The DA charged him with Liv's murder," Banks said.

James furrowed his brow. "How?"

"We found the murder weapon behind Frank's refrigerator. It's a beautiful pocketknife. Had a drop of Liv's blood inside the handle. Probably cost a fortune."

James loosened his tie, suddenly feeling restricted. He struggled to keep his voice even. "Do you think he'll be convicted?"

"There's a good chance, although Decker said something interesting." Banks paused for effect. "He said you trashed his house and planted the knife."

James sat at a student's desk in the front row, his legs suddenly wobbly. "That's crazy."

Detective Banks faced James, standing over him, studying him for a few seconds. "As a detective, I like to know everything. Maybe you're like that as a professor?"

"I'm not sure …" James trailed off.

"Decker said this happened on the first Monday in September, which interestingly was two weeks after we met about that cell phone you got from Leah Henderson. Remember that?"

James nodded. His underarms and lower back were sticky with sweat.

"Do you remember what you told me?"

James shook his head.

"You said, 'If you won't do your job, I will.'"

James swallowed hard.

"Another thing that's interesting is, three days before Decker claims that you trashed his house, you went to visit Damon Williams in prison." Banks waited for a reply that never came. "You know what I think?"

James cleared his throat. "No."

"I think Damon told you about Liv and Rachel and his theories about Decker. That and your lingering suspicions from the cell phone compelled you to break into Decker's house and to turn the place upside down, looking for evidence. I think you found that beautiful knife, and you saw the inscription that read, *Love always, RT*. I think it stands for Rachel Taylor. That's how I knew the knife wasn't yours. Rachel would've used RTH for Rachel Taylor-Harris if the knife was for you. I think that inscription made you mad enough to chew nails and spit rivets. So, you used that knife to rip his furniture to shreds. You finished in the basement and then chucked the knife against the wall. I think you meant to break the glass behind the bar, but you missed, and it fell behind the fridge. On your way out, I think you flooded the house somehow. I'm thinking you ran the hose." Banks raised one brow. "Am I right?"

James stared through Banks. "I don't know what you're talking about."

"We didn't find a single hair or fingerprint of yours in Decker's house. Luckily you wore gloves, or we'd be having a different conversation. Imagine if your fingerprints were on that knife instead of Frank's."

"I don't know what you're talking about," James repeated.

Banks frowned. "I was hoping you'd be more honest with me. I'd like to know if my theory's true."

"What do you want from me?"

"Normally, I'd be pissed about you potentially destroying and planting evidence, but, in this case, it was a stroke of dumb luck."

James leaned back in the chair and crossed his arms over his chest. "How so?"

"Decker never filed a police report or an insurance report, which made me wonder why? My first thought was that it never happened, but when I was reviewing Decker's finances, I noticed that he wrote a check to a contractor and rented something from an equipment rental place on the day after your break-in. I called the contractor and found out that he replaced the sliding glass door, which explains the glass shards I found on the back patio. Also explains your point of entry.

"I called the rental place too and found out that he rented industrial blowers for drying houses that have water damage." Banks nodded to himself. "I thought, the break-in did happen, but why didn't Decker file an insurance claim or a police report? The obvious answer is he didn't want anyone to know you had trashed his house, especially the police. Then Decker told Matt Taylor a story about how you abused Rachel and hired Damon to kill her. I think Decker hoped that Matt might do his dirty work for him. We both know how that went. Unfortunately, I can't prove intent beyond a reasonable doubt. Maybe if Matt had survived."

"You believe Decker tried to have me killed?" James asked.

"If Decker wanted you dead, why would he save your life? He could've easily let you drown in that quarry." Banks held up one finger. "That was one thing I couldn't figure out, until I thought back to that day, from a different perspective. When I made it to the shore of the quarry pond, I saw Decker in the water, but I didn't see you. When he saw me, he grabbed you and pulled you to shore. I think he was drowning you. Then when he saw me, he had to play the good cop. I think he thought you were dead anyway. I don't think he anticipated that I'd bring you back to life."

James nodded, thinking about that day at the quarry, vaguely remembering a big splash and someone holding him under water. "Where does this leave us?"

"With dumb luck. I think, after you ransacked his house, Decker noticed that his knife was gone and assumed you stole it. So, he doesn't think it's still in the house, which is exactly *why* it was still in the house when we searched it. I'm convinced he would have gotten rid of the knife prior to the search, if it would've been in its original space. *Dumb luck.* If you hadn't tossed that knife behind the fridge, we never would've found it, and Decker would've gotten away with murder."

"Do I need an attorney?" James asked.

Banks chuckled. "I could dig around. See where your cell phone was on the day in question. Talk to Decker's neighbors. See if they saw you at the scene. I might be able to make a case for breaking and entering, vandalism—but I'm retiring. Today's actually my last day." Banks checked his watch. "Technically, I'm retired as of seven minutes ago. Even if I wanted to make a case against you, that ship has sailed. To Florida to be precise. The wife and I are moving to the sunshine state. I've had enough of these winters." Banks reached into his pocket and removed a packet of Nicorette Gum. "My wife's been begging me to quit smoking for years." He popped a piece of gum into his mouth. "Finally took the plunge. This gum's nothing like my Newports, but I'd like to have a *long* retirement, if you know what I mean."

James stood from his seat. "Are you saying I'm in the clear?"

Detective Banks held out his hand. "That's exactly what I'm saying."

James shook the old detective's hand. "Thank you for everything."

"Just doing my job."

Banks turned and went to the door. He opened it.

James called out, "Detective Banks."

Banks pivoted back to James, standing in the doorway, half in and half out.

"I also tossed four dozen eggs around the house."

Banks laughed. "Have a nice life, James." The old detective left the classroom and his profession behind.

EPILOGUE

ANNA STOOD in front of the mirror in their bedroom, wearing only her underwear and her engagement ring, checking her stomach from the front, then the side. "I think I'm starting to show."

"Let's see." James slipped out of bed, wearing his boxer briefs. He took Anna's hands and turned her to face him, staring at her stomach. He ran his hands over her tiny baby bump. Then he knelt and kissed her stomach, sensual at first, then rapid and goofy.

She stepped back, giggling. "Stop it."

James grinned. "Sorry. One more kiss." He knelt before her again, kissed her baby bump, and said, "I love you."

She ran her hands through his hair.

He stood and kissed her on the lips. "I love *you* too."

"Are you sure we can do this?" she asked, biting the lower corner of her lip.

"*We*? I'm sure *you* can do it. If I had to birth a baby, we'd be in trouble."

Anna slapped him on the rear end. "You know what I mean."

"You'll be great. *We'll* be great. We'll have the smartest, most adorable child ever conceived."

Anna smirked. "That's what every parent says."

James kissed her on the cheek. "We're the only ones who will be right."

She smiled. "We are pretty cute and smart."

"Now you're talking. You hungry yet?"

"How about omelets?"

"Sounds good." James dressed in sweats and a fleece.

Anna went to the bathroom.

"I'll be in the kitchen," James called out to the bathroom, before leaving their master bedroom.

He didn't go to the kitchen though. He forgot to grab the mail on Friday, so he slipped on his sneakers and his coat, before stepping outside. His fruit trees were barren, having dropped their leaves two months ago. A cool breeze nipped at his ears. At the end of his long driveway, he opened the mailbox and removed five letters.

As he ambled back up the driveway, he flipped through the letters. *Junk, junk, bill, bill. What's this?* James stopped on the driveway and opened a letter from First National Insurance. He removed two trifolded pieces of paper from the envelope. The first one was a letter from First National, but he didn't read it. He was too transfixed on the second piece of paper. At the bottom of the second piece of paper was a check, to be detached at the perforation.

It was made payable to James Harris in the amount of $2,000,000.

―――

Death Do Us Part will continue in Book 2.

THANK YOU FOR READING DEATH DO US PART

WE HOPE you enjoyed it as much as we enjoyed bringing it to you. We just wanted to take a moment to encourage you to review the book. Follow this link: Death Do Us Part to be directed to the book's Amazon product page to leave your review.

Every review helps further the author's reach and, ultimately, helps them continue writing fantastic books for us all to enjoy.

———

Want to discuss our books with other readers and even the authors? Join our Discord server today and be a part of the Aethon community.

Facebook | Instagram | Twitter | Website

You can also join our non-spam mailing list by visiting www.subscribepage.com/AethonReadersGroup and never miss out on future releases. You'll also receive three full books completely Free as our thanks to you.

Looking for more great books?

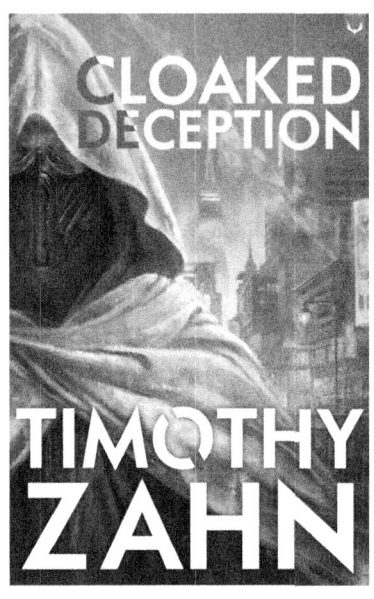

From Timothy Zahn, Hugo Award winner and #1 **New York Times** *bestselling author of* **Star Wars: Heir to the Empire,** *comes this pulse-pounding political thriller. A tactical nuclear weapon is stolen from an Indian research facility, setting off a chain of events that spans the globe. Those behind the heist plan to use it to take out thousands of innocent people—all to assure death of a single man who they believe is too dangerous to be left alive. What are the lives of thousands compared to the safety of the world? At the same time, scientists have invented the world's first cloaking device, able to render its user almost completely invisible. It's the epitome of hidden-in-plain-sight—a game changer for any military. At least until three of the lead scientists are murdered and their work is stolen the night before their first demonstration. Authorities have no idea the two crimes are connected. There are ten days before the bomb is set to go off. Can they unravel the trail of red herrings in time? The clock is ticking...* **The legendary Timothy Zahn, best-known for creating the popular Thrawn character last seen in** **Star Wars: Ahsoka,** *returns with this original, unputdownable thriller.* CLOAKED DECEPTION *is filled with twists and turns and a blistering conclusion you'll never see coming!*

Get Cloaked Deception now!

DEATH DO US PART 255

———

———

For all of our science fiction titles, check out www.aethonbooks.com/science-fiction

If you enjoyed this novel, … you'll love *Cesspool*.

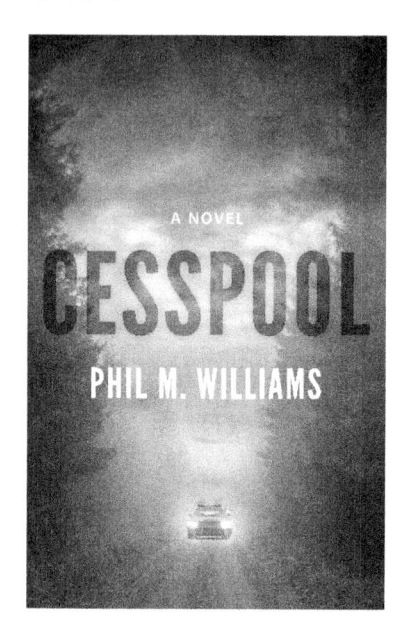

Click here for *Cesspool*:
Cesspool Amazon Link

Would you become a criminal to do the right thing?

Disgraced teacher, James Fisher, moved to a backwoods town, content to live his life in solitude. He was awakened from his apathy by a small girl with a big problem. James suspected Brittany was being abused and exploited by his neighbor. He called the police but soon realized his mistake, as the neighbor was related to the chief of police.

Most would've looked the other way. Getting involved placed James squarely in the crosshairs of the local police. James lacked the brawn or the connections to save himself, much less Brittany. The police held all the power, and they knew it. But that was also their weakness. They underestimated what the mild-mannered teacher and the young runaway would do for justice.

Buy *Cesspool* today if you enjoy vigilante justice page-turners with a side of underdog.

Adult language and content.

What Readers Are Saying

"Wow. Just wow. This book was amazing. Every chapter, every page had me thinking about ideas, philosophies, current events, history in a different way." - Elaine ★★★★★

"The writing is excellent, the pace quick, the characters and dialog believable. An excellent read." - Dusty Sharp, Author of the Austin Conrad Series ★★★★★

"I have enjoyed this author before, but this is his best yet. If you want a story that will keep you reading, this is it. The story, the characters, and the cunning displayed by the hero is some of the best fiction I've had the pleasure to read. Do yourself a favor and pick up this book. You won't lay it down until the end." - Patrick R. ★★★★★

"Wow! This was one of the best books I've read in a while. Twists, turns, and unexpected events in every chapter. What a movie this would make." – Kindle Customer ★★★★★

. . .

"This book was incredible! I read it in three days—the entire story is a whirlwind of fantastic characters, a perfect constancy of ups and downs throughout." - Rae L. ★★★★★

For the Reader

Dear Reader,

I'm thrilled that you took precious time out of your life to read my novel. Thank you! I hope you found it entertaining, engaging, and thought-provoking. If so, please consider writing a positive review on your favorite retail site. Five-star reviews have a huge impact on future sales. The review doesn't need to be long and detailed, if you're more of a reader than a writer. As an author and a small businessman, competing against the big publishers, I greatly appreciate every reader, every review, and every referral.

If you're interested in receiving two of my novels for free and/or reading my other titles for free or discounted, go to the following link: http://www.PhilWBooks.com. You're probably thinking, *What's the catch?* There is no catch.

If you want to contact me, don't be bashful. I can be found at Phil@PhilWBooks.com. I do my best to respond to all emails.

Sincerely,
Phil M. Williams

Gratitude

I'd like to thank my wife for being my first reader, sounding board, and cheerleader. I struggled with the complexity of this plot and bored her with endless possibilities of where to take the story. Her support, patience, and unwavering belief in my skill as an author was integral to the creation of this story. I love you, Denise.

I'd also like to thank my editors. My developmental editor, Caroline Smailes, did a fantastic job finding the holes in my plot and suggesting remedies. As always, my line editor, Denise Barker (not to be confused with my wife, Denise Williams), did a fantastic job making sure the manuscript was error-free. I love her comments and feedback.

Thank you to my mother-in-law, Joy, one of the best nurses on this planet. She is always gracious with her time and extremely knowledgeable about all things medical.

Thank you to my beta readers, Ray and Ann. They're my last defense against the dreaded typo. And thank you to you, the reader. Without you I wouldn't have a career. As long as you keep reading, I'll keep writing.